Time stopped and started again before Justin lifted his mouth from Amelia's

...She attempted to push away from him but his grip tightened, pulling her into an even closer embrace. She felt as though he was drinking the breath from her body, replacing it with an effervescent substance that bubbled in her veins and intoxicated her senses. She pressed against him, needing the strength of his muscular body to support her failing balance.

Breathless, hair tousled, cheeks flushed, Amelia began to pull away. "Justin, Justin...you must stop. Please, I must talk to you."

"I couldn't help myself...I must have you. I need you more than I've ever needed anyone before...."

Dear Reader:

We've had thousands of wonderful surprises at SECOND CHANCE AT LOVE since we launched the line in June 1981.

We knew we were going to have to work hard to bring you the six best romances we could each month. We knew we were working with a talented, caring group of authors. But we *didn't* know we were going to receive such a warm and generous response from readers. So the thousands of wonderful surprises are in the form of letters from readers like you who've been kind with your praise, constructive and helpful with your suggestions. We read each letter...and take it seriously.

It's been a thrill to ''meet'' our readers, to discover that the people who read SECOND CHANCE AT LOVE novels and write to us about them are so remarkable. Our romances can only get better and better as we learn more and more about you, the reader, and what you like to read.

So, I hope you will continue to enjoy SECOND CHANCE AT LOVE and, if you haven't written to us before, please feel free to do so. If you have written, keep in touch.

With every good wish,

Sincerely,

Carolyn Nichols

Carolyn Nichols
SECOND CHANCE AT LOVE
The Berkley/Jove Publishing Group
200 Madison Avenue
New York, New York 10016

P.S. Because your opinions *are* so important to us, I urge you to fill out and return the questionnaire in the back of this book.

Second Chance at Love
REGENCY

LOVE'S MASQUERADE
LILLIAN MARSH

**SECOND CHANCE AT LOVE
BOOK**

LOVE'S MASQUERADE

First edition published May 1982

First printing

"Second Chance at Love" and the butterfly emblem are trademarks belonging to Jove Publications, Inc.

Printed in the United States of America

Second Chance at Love books are published by
The Berkley/Jove Publishing Group
200 Madison Avenue, New York, NY 10016

To my sister Sara
with love.

LOVE'S
MASQUERADE

PROLOGUE

"IT'S INDECENT, THAT'S what it is . . . you, dressing yourself like some Cyprian, getting ready to bed yourself with a stranger. Your mother would turn in her grave if she knew."

"Annie, not another word about it. I won't have you biting at me like this." The beautiful young woman leaned forward to inspect the black beauty mark she had just placed to the left of her exquisitely curved lips. "Please, my love, don't keep on at me. I need your confidence, not your scolding. Looking like a Cyprian for a few nights will be a small price to pay to be able to give Alfred the child he wants. He has been so good to us . . . so good to me. This is the only way I can repay him." She paused for a moment, then in a whisper added, "I'm frightened enough . . . but I know I'm right."

The older woman continued grumbling as she helped her

mistress attach a small arrangement of feathers and flowers to her coiffure. The reflection in the mirror showed a delicate oval face lit by tilted eyes the color of the ocean under a stormy sky. Curls of a tawny, almost apricot color sprang from a smooth, white brow. A straight nose above a mouth made sensuous by a slightly full lower lip completed the perfection of her face—a perfection that was relieved from being boring by the twinkle of dimples that appeared when she smiled.

Apparently satisfied with her looks, the young woman, who appeared to be about three and twenty, stood and lifted her arms to allow her dresser to drop a froth of lace over her head and set it in place on her body. She swirled around to get the effect of the movement of her full-skirted ball gown. Although her hair was unpowdered, her appearance in this year of 1814 was that of a belle of an earlier year. The shimmering satin underskirt of *eau de Nile* was covered by a pale ecru overdress of the finest chantilly lace, gathered and ruched in panniers designed to emphasize its wearer's tiny waist. The moment she stood still again, Annie gave a tug to the top of the low-cut bodice that barely covered the woman's white breasts.

"Annie, what are you doing?"

"I'm atryin' to make you look less indecent, ye shameless hussy." Annie's voice had become more shrill as she became more upset. "The master will love ye jist as well with or without a child. Look what we're adoing to yersel', m'dearie. 'Tis not right!"

The begowned girl took pity on her maid's anguish and soothed her with gentle pats.

"Ah, Annie, Annie . . . you can't have forgotten how much I owe my husband. If I can give him the child he longs for, should I not try? If not for him, I might truly have had to resort to the life of a lightskirt. What else was there for me at the age of seventeen, with both parents dead, no money, and no relatives to take me in?"

Softly Amelia Farrow Carrington reminded Annie of the debt she felt she owed to her husband, Alfred. When, at the age of seventeen, her father and sole remaining parent had died, Carrington had taken pity on her and presented her with a comfortable, orderly life filled with love and caring. Her father and he had been friends, incongruous as it now seemed. The relationship between the charming wastrel who was her parent and the scholarly man who had become her husband had been one of long standing. They had known each other at Oxford and found something to like about each other that kept them in touch throughout the changes in their lives. Both men were of excellent background but had chosen different paths, Amelia's father becoming a gambler who spent his entire inheritance at the tables, Alfred Carrington a learned man whose knowledge of Elizabethan literature made him one of the leading experts in his field. As a result of his success, as well as his financial and social eligibility, he was able to help Amelia's father over the years. At Peter Farrow's death in a racing accident, Carrington, as a close friend of the family, came forward to help the bereft Amelia through the trials of selling off her father's holdings and settling what debts remained.

During the several weeks after the funeral, Carrington's gentle manner and understanding, his restraint and affection made Amelia's life more secure and more manageable than it had ever been. When the older man asked her to marry him, she accepted. Though they did not share the passionate love she had hoped to find for herself, she felt cared for and protected, and returned her husband's love with gratitude and affectionate regard.

Unfortunately, in the six years that they had been married, she had not conceived a child. Alfred was thirty years older than she and the doctors she had consulted said that he could no longer father children. So, without telling him, she had decided, after long thought, to find a substitute to father her child. Alfred need never know. It would be her gift to him. The real father of the child would never know either.

Amelia's thoughts were interrupted by Annie asking her why she had chosen to meet this particular man.

"This Justin Farnham now, how did you decide on him? Tell me again and maybe I'll be understanding how you could do such a thing. Oh my, oh my ... I'll not be able to face yer mother when I meet her in the afterlife."

"Annie, my love, stop your caterwauling. You'll wake the whole house, even my husband, though he's in Italy." Amelia pulled Annie to a sofa and sat down beside her. "This Justin Farnham is the most sought-after bachelor in London—no, I might say in England. I told you about his work with the foreign office and his friendship with the prime minister. Why do you keep wanting to hear about him? Not that I don't want to talk about him." For a moment Amelia's shoulders slumped and her voice was stilled. Then, with a toss of her tawny head, she straightened her back. "But you and I, Annie dearest, know that even though I am going to bed another man, I am still faithful to my husband."

"I know, my lamb, I know." The abigail took the young woman's hands in hers. "Tell me again, not about his work, but what he's like as a man. I want to feel that you will be safe, my lovely." Annie held Amelia's hands in a tight grip.

Before she answered, Amelia remembered the first time she'd seen Justin Farnham. She had been walking down the high street in Oxford one day during Alfred's tenure there, when her eye had been caught by a dashing equipage drawn by two perfectly matched dappled-gray geldings. The curricle was at a standstill in the crush of traffic on the road, which gave her time to study its occupants. The woman in the carriage had been obviously not-quite-polite society, but the gentleman was certainly a top-of-the-trees gallant. His smile had been wicked as he laughed at something his companion had said. His aquiline features—the angular, high cheekbones and proud, straight nose—were contradicted by his mobile, sensuous mouth. His attire had been of the best and his manner a combination of ease and pride that had attracted Amelia's interest enough so that he had remained in her memory. In the three years since then, she had glimpsed him briefly once more and learned from an acquaintance that he was Justin Farnham, Earl of Croyville. Something about him had stimulated her imagination. Perhaps it had been an instinctive response to the "catch-me-if-you-can" challenge that an autocratic male frequently, albeit unknowingly, seemed to offer.

"All right, I'll tell you once more. He's first of all intelligent, well-connected, of the nobility. He is a Corinthian, a Nonesuch. He's handsome, of the right age—thirtyish, I think—and is well-educated. He's well liked by the ladies and has the reputation of being an accomplished flirt and a good provider for those with whom he no longer conducts *les petites liaisons*. He's supposed to be close-mouthed, and he's well-spoken. And according to one of his past mistresses, he is considerate in bed." By now covered with blushes, Amelia dropped a kiss on Annie's cheek.

Annie let out a wail. "And who would the shameless piece of muslin be who gave ye such an opinion?"

"I overheard two ladies speaking to each other and comparing experiences. They didn't even know I was listening." Amelia smiled at her maid. "But it *is* important to know, isn't it? I wouldn't want to bed a man who would be cruel or . . . or . . . well, you've heard stories just as I have, haven't you? And I'd be a fool to choose that kind of man as the father of my child."

"No matter what yer reasoning, I'll not like the whole thing. I thank the good St. Patrick your husband is away. If he should ever learn of what ye're to do, it will be the death of him. And him such a good man. Oh, be careful my Mellikin." Annie threw her apron over her head to cover her tears. "I'll have Staunton put the horses to. He'll probably have the carriage waiting to leave with ye."

Within minutes the marked young woman was on her way to Vaux Hall Pleasure Gardens. She had chosen this evening in particular because the event was a *bal masqué*. The beginning movement of her seduction of Justin Farnham, Earl of Croyville and a beau of the first order, was made to allow the secrecy of her mask to have validity. Once he accepted the mask, she would make it a rule. He must never learn her true identity.

She hoped she was not being too optimistic. If there were no child, the whole would have been for naught. To a woman of Amelia's high principles, the betrayal of her husband would have been unthinkable were it not for the fact that she had no other way to give him the child he so desired.

Too soon, Staunton announced their arrival at the dock-side for the ferry to Vaux Hall. He insisted upon accompanying her on the short river trip to the pleasure gardens. "I'll await you here, mistress," he announced. "If you have other company on the trip back, I will see you safely on your way and then return home. You needn't worry that I will give you away, but I must see you are safe." He looked at her, this middle-aged, upright man who had been taking care of her household since she was a child. "If there were any way to convince your foolish head that this is a dangerous thing you're doing, believe me, I'd do it. But I understand your need to please Mr. Carrington, strange a way as it may seem to others. I will wish you good luck, my dear lady."

The trip by ferry took but a short while. At the boatslip Amelia threw her arms around Staunton in a tight hug, whispering a soft, "Thank you." She adjusted the frilly lace edge of the *eau de Nile* mask covering the upper portion of her face and, with a determined step, she walked through the great gateway and into the lantern-lit aisle that led to the rotunda of the gardens. The crowds were not as thick as they would be in another hour; she would find it easier to spot her quarry this way. She had paid well to learn that the earl would be an early arrival at the fete this evening.

She had almost reached the end of the path when she saw him walking to the side and somewhat ahead of her. A quiver of fear ran through her at the thought of what she was about to do; the sight of the tall figure was almost enough to make her change her mind.

The man wore a blue-black domino but had not yet raised the hood. Keeping her eye on his direction, Amelia took a crosswalk that would bring her out a few steps in front of him. As she stepped back into the main walk, she glanced to her rear to make sure she was located just a stride in front of her "seducer." With a sigh of relief, she realized he hadn't noticed her maneuvering. She heard his footsteps behind her; she stopped, then turned, causing him to run right into her.

The earl had been walking in a brown study, wondering

why he had allowed himself to be inveigled into another such evening of mindless fun. Life was becoming too boring to think about. Deep in thought, his eyes were watching the pathway immediately in front of his feet. Suddenly his breath was knocked from him by a body stumbling against his. He reached out automatically to prevent the unknown person from falling and was pleased to feel the bare skin of a woman's shoulders. He heard a gasp and then the stutter of an apology. Slowly he raised his eyes from two dainty feet in green slippers to shadowed eyes behind a green mask. He stepped backward, allowing his hands to slide down his assailant's arms to her hands. Lingeringly he let his eyes take in her exquisitely formed mouth, her soft white shoulders and rounded breasts exposed by the deep décolletage of her dress of the *ancien régime*.

The flat planes of his lean cheeks were creased in a lazy smile that almost touched his eyes. "And what have we here? I beg your pardon, Madame—du Barry?—if I have upset you or caused you to hurt yourself."

The breathtaking young woman swayed toward him, never taking her eyes from his. She could feel his strength in the grip of his hands as he held hers. Amelia quelled the frisson of fear that fluttered through her and began to enact her role of a lady of few morals. She smiled slightly and lifted her head, arching her back to better display her beautiful breasts. Then, in an accent that was recognizably French, she began to apologize for causing the handsome gentleman such inconvenience . . . but then, perhaps it was fate that had brought them together because, if she was not mistaken, he was Justin Farnham. "And, m'sieu, I have been waiting all my life to meet you."

Farnham's eyes gleamed in appreciation—this encounter promised to enliven the boredom of the evening.

"Allow me then, madame, to hear your name. You flatter me but hold me at a disadvantage." The earl raised her hand to his lips. "Will you walk with me while you tell me why you have waited so long to make my acquaintance?"

Amelia flirted her fan at the attractive Farnham. "My name shall be . . . Mystère . . . and my story—ah, that also is a mystery. It will take too long to tell standing here. Shall we walk awhile first, m'sieu, for is this not the lover's walk?"

The earl studied the masked face before him. The girl's manner was provocative but not in the ordinary way. She was no lightskirt out for a mark but a damned attractive piece. This should be an enjoyable interlude. If the rest of her face matched her lips and her body, she was truly an incomparable.

With a careless shrug of his broad shoulders, Farnham tucked Amelia's hand in his arm and answered, "By all means, my lady Mystère, let us walk and perhaps later will follow wine and . . . talk."

CHAPTER ONE

THE SHEER BLACK-SILK veil did little to hide the beautiful young widow's simply dressed tawny hair. She sat in a high-backed chair, her head resting against the intricate petitpoint pattern. The unrelieved black of her gown and the severe head covering indicated that her loss had been recent. In fact, the lawyer, Ugo Beneventi, was at that moment reading Alfred Carrington's last will and testament. As *Avvocato* Beneventi's Italian tenor droned on, Amelia let her mind relive the last few years. She contemplated the quiet happiness of her twelve-year marriage to Carrington. He had been so loving and so understanding; the shelter of his love had been the mainstay of her existence.

The sound of the lawyer's voice speaking her name and the name of her son, Peregrine, brought Amelia out of her reverie. But it was just the continuing enumeration of bequests. She sank back into her remembrances. Peregrine, her adorable little boy, the child whose birth had given Alfred such deep pleasure. The child who was the son of Justin Farnham, but who had been brought up as the son of Alfred Carrington. Had her husband known the truth? Amelia wondered. At times she had thought he guessed her deception, but he had never shown any displeasure or expressed doubt about Peregrine. He had never known about Justin Farnham, never known of the wild and thrilling passion that had come to her in that brief affair. If her love and respect had not been so strong, if she had not felt so grateful to Alfred, it would have been easy to succumb to the ecstasy she had found in Justin's arms. So easy to have given up her husband for the man who had taught her the limitless pleasures her body could know.

She never told her lover the real reason for their affair, that she wanted a child to give her husband. She never told Farnham her name, nor had he ever seen her face. Somehow she had intrigued him the more by insisting on secrecy. She gave him her body but not her identity. Even in their most passionate bouts of love, she had worn the mask. He knew every pore of her body but not her face. Never would he recognize her and jeopardize her relationship with her husband.

She had wanted to continue their affair as long as he showed interest, but she had begun to respond to him in a way that she found shocking. Shocking because she was not only swept to heights of physical pleasure that she had never attained as Alfred's wife, but also because she had begun to enjoy his mind and his presence. By the fourth time they had met, she was almost totally enamoured of him. And so she decided to end it before she lost her sanity and became his totally, to the detriment of her marriage and her self. That was the last time they had met, the last time she had known the consummate artistry of his passion.

Fortunately, Alfred had already left for Padua to make arrangements for her arrival at a later date; he was not witness to her sleepless nights and drawn face. He did not see her grieving for the man who was her other half, the sun to her moon. She had thanked God that she would be out of England for the next few years. She would never have been able to meet Justin without giving way to her feelings. But she was rewarded. She had conceived and was able to present Alfred with a beautiful baby boy.

It had been seven years since last she and Justin had been together, but still the thought of his hand on her body, his lips on her throat, his long, lean length next to her, was enough to cause her breath to stop. His skilled body had taught her carnal love; his brilliant mind had stimulated an intellectual love—a devastating combination.

Amelia had shown a strength and maturity that was beyond most young women, especially at three and twenty, her age at the time of her affair. And though her heart wept in secret, her grief lessened when she saw Alfred's joy and love for his son. For Perry was his son, even though it had not been his seed that had sired the boy. The child adored the father even as the father worshiped the boy. From the day of his birth, he had become the center of Carrington's existence and the receptacle for his love and wisdom. The love that had been given to Amelia expanded to take in her child.

The next few years were halcyon years. Alfred's success in Padua, the love they both felt for the child and each other, and the magic that seemed to result from this love created a gentle, tender shelter that gave succor to all who came within its reach. The elderly professor and his young, beautiful wife were a beloved couple who, strangely, in a country of passionate love affairs, were never leered at or sneered at for the difference in their ages. They had a quality that was a confirmation of goodness and love and that gave pleasure to all who were touched by their presence.

This gentle existence came to an end with the onset of Alfred's illness. It was of short duration, a mere four months, but long enough for him to make specific plans for Amelia's future. Parts she had made mild objections to, but on the whole she accepted Alfred's wisdom and decisions. Because of the way he expressed himself—especially his gratitude—she felt he may have been aware that Perry was not actually his child, but he never faced her with an accusation or an unspoken condemnation. She would miss him bitterly, no matter what turn her life might take. He would always be a most beloved part of her life, a part that she held to with no regrets.

Once again Amelia's reverie was interrupted, this time by the cessation of the lawyer's voice. She became aware that the gathered servants and the *avvocato* were looking at her, waiting for her to speak.

"Signor Beneventi," she began gracefully, "you have given such attention to helping the family Carrington in this time of trouble. My husband would have appreciated it greatly."

"O cara signora, it was the least I could do for so good a friend. It is the least I can do for one so young and lovely:" The paunchy little lawyer bowed carefully to the widow.

"My husband suggested that we go to Genoa and from there by ship. Since we will not be traveling until the late spring or early summer, the voyage should be an easy one."

"Dearest lady, you may rely upon me for your travel passes and any other small services I may perform for you. Don't let yourself become too lonely in your widowhood. There are many who love you dearly, as I do, and would do everything in their power to make your life a little . . . more comfortable. Gracious lady"—the lawyer received his hat from the attentive Staunton—"permit me to kiss your hand. I am your servant." Bowing deeply, the lawyer left in a flurry of poetic expressions, repeating his offers of undying service.

The closing of the great hall door was a signal for Amelia to collapse on the upholstered bench beside the door to the morning room. Covering her face to stifle her giggles, she rocked with laughter at the knightly promises of the corpulent, slightly ridiculous lawyer. The cleansing effect of the laughter swept away the depression that had held her in its grip since the moment she had learned her husband was dying. She had had to hide her anguish from her son and her husband. Only Annie knew of the hours of weeping she had suffered.

Her husband had astonished her with his acceptance of his coming end. He had astonished her too with the way he had immediately begun to make plans for her future. He planned every step of the next two years precisely, clearly, and with a specific end in mind. He had decided that the best thing for her to do would be to use her inheritance to find herself a wealthy husband. It was of the utmost importance to him that Perry have a father to love and care for him. Carrington's greatest hope was that Amelia would find someone to love her whom she could love in return, but it was as important, if not more so, that she respect her future husband. When Alfred Carrington had told her his plans and schooled her in the details of handling the funds he was to leave her, she'd been hard put to control her emotions. She scarcely knew whether to laugh at the impossibility of a man choosing his own successor or to cry at his earnest endeavor to plan her future.

Now, even though she had doubts about it, she ought to begin to put Alfred's plan into action. She had acceded to his advice in those last few months because he was dying, and she'd had no wish to mar his peace with brangling.

She allowed a few days to go by in order to recover from the exigencies of the funeral and condolence calls. Then, one wintry morning, she summoned Annie and Staunton to her chamber and took the first step toward her new life.

"You have both been with me since I was a child," she began as she studied the two people who were her only family besides her son. They knew her as well as she knew herself. Annie had nursed her through measles and a broken arm and countless colds when she was a child. Staunton had taught her to ride, to take her fences with all her heart and courage, and to look trouble straight in the eye. He had told her of her parents' death and comforted her immediately afterward. Both of them, she knew, were as loyal to her as she was to herself. They, in all the world, were the only ones who knew the truth about Perry. And they were indispensible to the plan's success.

"I know my husband told you of his wishes before he died, and as much as I find it difficult to think so coldly about the efforts we will have to make to find a successor for him—" Suddenly Amelia began to cry; the tears she had repressed poured forth, shaking her body with sobs. "I don't want another husband . . . but I promised him, I promised him. Oh, Annie, what shall I do?"

Quickly, the maid moved to her side, taking Amelia into her arms. "There, there, my lamb, let the tears come. It's about time you gave in to your sadness. But he was right, y'know. Perry will be needing a pa and you are much too young to be without a husband for long. 'Tis a passionate woman ye are, and he was knowing of that and wished for your happiness as well as that of the boy."

A rumble of agreement came from the stolid Staunton. "You know you're going to follow his wishes, Miss Melly." The use of the name he had called her as a child brought fresh tears to Amelia's eyes. "Now, it's enough with the tears. You've a great adventure to be starting on, and the sooner we get to it the better. Why, we'll be happy as grigs to get back to our own country, you'll see. You'll love it once we're back." He patted her hands with a clumsy affection.

Amelia dried her eyes and her mouth twisted in a miniature smile, although her glistening green eyes were still sad. "So foolish, I don't know what came over me. Suddenly the whole thing . . . the whole idea of moving to England, taking a house, meeting people . . . all without Alfred, just seemed too much. But you're right, dear Staunton. It will be an adventure. That's what he wanted it to be. And that's what we'll make it." With determination, the widow, now in full control of herself, sat up straight in her chair and motioned to her two servants to sit down with her.

"The first thing we have to do, Staunton, is to arrange for you to travel to London. We must have a home to go to and a proper address. Alfred said we should be near Grosvenor Square, if possible. He mentioned Princess Gardens as suitable. You'll have to get in touch with his man of business—Mr. Plimpton. He'll know just what I want; he's already been notified. And the hiring of servants . . ."

And so Amelia and her two *aides-de-camp* put in motion Alfred Carrington's plan. Without her realizing it, a rising excitement swept through the young woman. For the first time in her twenty-nine years she would be responsible only to herself. Now, finally she would make her mark on the world.

CHAPTER TWO

"PERRY! PERRY! WHERE has that child got to? Perry!" Annie's voice soared over the chatter of the footman putting the last pieces of luggage aboard the coach. The courtyard in front of the Carrington home was a scene of constant motion. The great coach, hitched up to six horses, was several feet higher than normal thanks to the abundance of satchels, bandboxes, and various clothing bags. Drawn up behind the coach and still being loaded or tied up were three wagons bulging with household furnishings, trunks filled with linens, draperies, small treasures, and crated paintings. Maids were rushing about lifting baskets of food into the coach. In addition to food for the trip to Genoa, one must take provisions to augment the fare prepared in the ship's galley during the voyage.

Amelia Carrington appeared in the doorway, holding her

excited son by the hand. Cautioning him to remain where he was, she walked over to Staunton, who was examining the lashings that secured the contents of one of the wagons to the framework.

"We'll be able to load these wagons right onto the ship, Miss Melly," the major-domo explained. "It saves time and makes for easier storage aboard the vessel. When we get to England, we'll have to hire horses to pull them to London, but that's a sight easier than trying to take our own horses with us. I've already arranged to sell these at the port. A dealer is giving us a good price for the stock."

"*Signora*, if you would please, your attention is needed over here." One of the manservants led the window to the front door of the villa. "Giovanni wants to present you with the present from all of us. We will miss you, mistress." In rapid Italian the attendant thanked Amelia for the years of kindness she had shown all who worked for her. With smiles and tears, the women and men who had taken care of the Carrington family during the happy years they had spent in Padua came up to Amelia to speak their farewells. Much moved by the affection and appreciation displayed by her staff, the young widow, now clad in gray half mourning, was hard put to accept their good wishes without breaking down. When they presented her with a gaily wrapped package, her emotions overcame her and she gave way to tears.

"Open it . . . open it, Mama." Perry danced about, begging to see what was in the box.

Carefully Amelia untied the bows and unwrapped the present. As she lifted the lid, she gasped in wonder at the exquisite embroidery.

"It is so you will never forget Padua and us, *ma donna*. We give you our love with this work of love."

Trying to control her tears, Amelia turned the huge bronze key in the door, feeling as she did so that she was locking away her life with Alfred. She caught Perry up in her arms. "Say good-bye now, Perry. It's time for us to be on our way." She handed the child up to Annie, who was already inside the coach, and then climbed in herself.

Staunton closed the coach door and climbed up on the

box next to the driver. "Let's go before they drown us with all the tears." His voice was a bit husky as he signaled to the drivers of the slowly moving wagons. "Follow closely. We make our first stop at noon."

They spent the next few days traveling to Genoa. Each evening they stopped for the night at an inn. On his return from London the month before, Staunton had made all the arrangements for their comfort. Annie would bustle into the rooms reserved for the party, giving orders for the stripping of the beds and the placement of valises. Then she would remake the beds with soft linens from the boxes they carried with them.

"I don't trust any of these innkeepers outside of England," she told Amelia. "Who knows what sort of riffraff have used the beds before we arrived? At least I know my bed linens have been cleaned well, and I can inspect the mattresses."

Each evening, before Perry was put to bed, he would ask questions about their new home. To the five-year-old, Italy was the known and familiar; England was a place that his father and mother had pictured for him in the stories they had told.

And each evening, as she answered his questions, Amelia would examine the child's face for traces of his real father. The memory of Justin Farnham was as vivid as though she had seen him just a short time ago. In her bed at night, her body remembered the thrill that his touch had brought her; her lips remembered his kisses. If only there were some way to relive those moments. But she must be wary. He must not ever find out how she had used him. A man of his pride could make a relentless enemy. Better to put all thought of her lost love away.

At last they reached the port of Genoa. Staunton was able to conduct them directly to the dock where the ship they were to travel on was at anchor. After the long trip from Padua, the hustle and bustle of the active port city was an exciting change.

Annie clung to Perry's legs as he leaned out the window of the coach, awestruck with the strange sights he beheld:

sailors in striped jerseys, occasionally with a gold earring in the ear, hand-drawn trucks laden with odd-looking vegetables, hawkers calling their wares, ship after ship lined up at the waterfront, and small boats traveling about the harbor, some with sails and some rowed by men stripped to the waist. The sounds of voices calling out commands or announcing their wares created a terrible noise. Perry's twin greyhounds and white macaw added their voices to the din.

Atop the coach, Staunton gave directions to the driver who brought the travelers directly to the side of the ship upon which they were to embark. Perry's mouth dropped open and his eyes grew huge at the sight of the vessel that would carry him to England.

Almost before the coach was brought to a halt, Staunton appeared at the window. "I would advise ye to remain in the coach until I check with the ship's officer, Miss Melly. There's such a hullabaloo going on about us that I would lose ye before I turned around." The fatherly retainer winked at Perry and cautioned him against falling out the coach window. "For ye'd go splat and we'd never be able to pick ye up again. And how would ye like that, hey?"

"Annie's holding on to my legs too hard, Staunton. She won't let me fall. Will you, Annie?" Perry laughed at Annie, who began to scold him for being a rambunctious little scamp.

"I can hardly believe we're on our way," Amelia murmured to Annie. "It hasn't seemed real until just now. It's all so much more exciting than I remember."

Amelia peered through the other window, as excited as her son about the embarkation. Her life was changing so rapidly. The smooth stream of days that had been their Padua experience was ended. Within the next two months she would be taking up a life she had never known before, that of a lady of fashion in one of the most exciting cities in the world—London. Her legacy from Alfred would be enough to give her two years in the highest kick of life. She could spend it all; Perry's inheritance was separate from hers and would not be touched.

"Mama, Mama, here comes Staunton with someone in a uniform. Oh my, he looks so fine. Do you think he's a captain?"

"We'll find out in a moment, dearest. Sit quietly until we're presented to the gentleman."

The door to the coach was opened by Staunton, who extended his arm to help Amelia alight from the vehicle. "Ma'am, I've brought First Officer Ardmore. He's to conduct ye aboard and show ye to your cabin."

As Amelia stepped down from the coach, her green eyes smiling, the tall young man bowed and said, "Your servant, ma'am. If you would be so kind as to follow me—"

"I'm Peregrine Carrington and this is my mother and this is Annie." Perry had jumped from the coach and addressed himself to the officer. "She's coming with us. Will you be able to put all our wagons on board? Is my pony going to come along? What do you call that thing that the men are walking on to get on the ship?"

"Perry, take a breath and let Officer Ardmore take us on board." Amelia laughed as she took her son's hand. "Please excuse him, Mr. Ardmore. He's so excited about traveling on such an elegant craft. I think I shall have to tie him to the mast to make sure he doesn't get into trouble."

"Don't be concerned, ma'am. We all get excited on sailing day. The voyage home, you know." The officer guided Amelia to the gangplank and steadied her as she stepped up it, Perry hanging tightly to her hand.

Once Perry had seen the cabin that he was to share with his mother and Annie, he danced with impatience to be taken up on deck to watch the loading. Excited herself at the prospect of finally being aboard, Amelia quickly wrapped herself in a shawl and conducted her son to the scene of frantic effort. Clutching Perry's hand, she tried to explain some of the various activities to the child. Her knowledge was limited, and she was soon unable to answer the boy's specific questions. Thus she was grateful to hear a deep voice answer his impatient question about the ship's sails and rigging.

"The boy seems to have the makings of a fine sailor,

ma'am," the gentleman addressed Amelia when she turned to see who possessed the voice instructing her son. "I hope you don't mind my answering his questions."

"Oh, no, you have relieved me of my heaviest burden," said the young woman with a laugh. "I could never bear to appear muddleheaded, so you have saved my vanity!"

"Allow me to believe that you could never appear muddleheaded. You are aware when you have not the answers, which is a great sign of intelligence" was the gentleman's smiling response. "May I take this opportunity to introduce myself? I am one of your fellow passengers, Sir Richard Dyckman."

"How do you do, Sir Richard." Amelia bowed her head in acknowledgment. "I am Amelia Carrington, and this is my son, Peregrine. Are you traveling to London also?"

"Yes. Fortunately my business is not too urgent, so I plan to enjoy this trip. I know the captain of our ship, John Englander, who is understood to be one of the best mariners for this type of run. We should have a good voyage. This time of year the weather is usually very fine. Have you traveled by water before?"

As he spoke, Sir Richard was taking Amelia's measure. He saw before him a woman in her late twenties of exceptional beauty. He was not much in the petticoat line, but this woman was unusual. He wondered where her husband was. By rights he should be the one answering the lively boy's questions.

". . . and so we decided to go by ship," Amelia finished. When she realized Sir Richard was gazing at her with a somewhat abstracted air, she called his name and woke him from reverie. "Now, why have you become so pensive, Sir Richard? Here you began by flattering me for my intelligence, and then you turn around and don't even hear my conversation. What shall I think?"

"Think only that I am a boor, Mrs. Carrington, not that it is any lack in you." Gracefully, the man excused himself to see to his cabin arrangements, leaving Amelia rather puzzled at his abrupt behavior. But she quickly forgot his manner when Annie and Staunton arrived to inform her that the Carrington wagons and animals were loaded. As the three adults and the child stood together observing the activities taking place on the lower deck, they heard commands to prepare for casting off. Perry's antics at this exciting news were enough to make his mother beg Staunton to keep the boy from casting himself overboard in his excitement.

The grizzled major-domo and the eager youngster settled themselves in a protected corner where they would be out of the way of the hustling sailors but were able to watch everything. With a feeling of relief, Amelia was free to move to the foredeck, where she could observe the sailing. She was filled with excitement—a combination of fear and anticipation—as she contemplated her life in London.

CHAPTER THREE

THE LIGHT FLICKERED as the overhead lamp swung in response to the ship's movement. The soft talk and laughter of the several people gathered about the dinner table was interspersed with offers of more food or wine from the stewards attending the diners. The distant snap of canvas and the creaking of the boat accompanied the sounds of the dinner party. Captain Englander had invited his passengers and several of his officers to his cabin. At present he was reminding Mrs. Carrington that she had promised to entertain the company with some songs.

Signor Pacelli, another passenger who had embarked at Genoa accompanied by his wife, was deep in a discussion with the captain about the new looms that had been introduced in the English wool manufactures. A tinkle of laughter came from Lady Brampton, who was carrying on a mild flirtation with the ship's first officer, Mr. Ardmore, and was trying to attach Sir Richard Dyckman.

Amelia looked around her at these new friends; young and old, they had drawn together despite differences in class and background. As she contemplated the various guests, Sir Richard turned to her with a question about her home in London.

"Staunton was able to arrange a very suitable lease for a house in Princess Gardens. My husband had given instructions before he . . . he . . ." Amelia still could not speak of Alfred's death with equanimity. "My man went to London months ago to make all the arrangements. We shall be able to go directly from the ship to our home. I hope, Sir Richard, that we can look forward to your paying us a call."

"But of course, dear lady." The handsome baronet smiled.

Amelia could hardly miss the admiration in Sir Richard's eyes. As she made desultory conversation with him, she looked intently at the man. Since they had set sail, he had been ever helpful. His patience with Perry, his gentle courtesy, his unfailing good humor had done a great deal to make the trip enjoyable. She guessed he was close to fifty years of age, if not a bit past that. His brown hair was just touched with white in the thick sideburns he affected. His brown eyes had a look of understanding and kindness that did not detract from the strength of his tall figure and broad shoulders. He was well dressed without being recognizably of any particular fashion group. In truth, he reminded her very much of Alfred, which was both good and bad. If she were to follow the plan, she must look upon him as good "husband" material. But if, as she was becoming more wont to do, she ignored that program, he could be a good friend. More and more she was feeling the need to direct her own destiny.

"And what have I done to earn such a searching regard, madam?" Dyckman laughingly inquired. "I seem to have sent you to another world."

"Oh, how bird-witted you will think me. I must have looked asleep with my eyes wide open. I was just thinking of the magnitude of the steps I am taking." Amelia lifted her wine glass to take a sip. "D'you know, for all my years, I have never been on my own before. It frightens me, but it also fills me with elation that at last I shall learn something new about myself. Shall I succeed or not? Do you understand what I mean?" She looked at Sir Richard with a question in her green eyes.

"I think I do, although I never really gave thought to a woman having such feelings. I think most men who must leave home and start a new venture, no matter what kind, have thoughts like that. It's a big step. You are very brave, Mrs. Carrington, to take your life into your own keeping like this. It's more usual for a widow to look for another husband as fast as possible." Sir Richard's cynicism surprised Amelia; sharing the feeling of surprise was mild embarrassment at the thought that she *was*, in truth, a widow planning a campaign to find a husband.

Again she wished she had given Alfred more of a battle over his plan. This idea that she would have to cold-heartedly choose a potential suitor and create the opportunities to be courted repelled her. Though she had given her promise to a dying man, she felt more and more inclined to break her word.

The steward interrupted her musing with an offer for more wine, which she refused. Suddenly impatient to leave, she rose and suggested that the women retire to the main saloon, leaving the men to their port and cigars.

As the other women withdrew, Amelia walked out onto the deck. The ship was moving well on a calm sea. She stood at the rail watching the ship's wake rippling in the moonlight. She had no idea of the beautiful figure she presented to the man who had followed her from the dining saloon. Richard Dyckman paused in the doorway to enjoy the sight of her graceful form. The thrust of her breasts above the delicate curve of her stomach, the shapeliness of her thighs—all were revealed by the steadily moving night air. Dyckman caught his breath. He had been a bachelor for many years, in fact had intended never to marry, but here was one woman who might be worthy of consideration. She would be the perfect wife for a diplomat. Her poise and beauty would be a credit to him wherever he served. Her manner was natural and easy with all, even while she retained the dignity inherent in her bearing. He supposed she had not thought of him in the role of a suitor, nor was he ready to approach her as such. However, he would think about it.

He moved to her side, draping the shawl he carried around her shoulders. "You left your wrap in the saloon, madam, and the night air can turn chilly."

"You are thoughtful, Sir Richard. Now that you mention it, I've begun to feel the cold. It's such a glorious night. Who would have thought that the stars could look so close." Amelia brought the shawl close about her as she spoke. "I always find it astonishing to think that the mariners can sail by the stars. How do they know which ones to watch?"

Dyckman began to point out various stars to Amelia, recounting some of the ancient tales told by countless generations of storytellers to explain the various constellations. He was still speaking about the belt of Orion when they heard Maria Waxrich, one of the passengers, calling Amelia's name.

"Oh, Mrs. Carrington." The young woman moved out of the passageway toward the pair. "The captain has asked us to do our duet now. Oh"—her voice faded in embarrassment—"I didn't mean to interrupt you . . ."

"My dear girl, you haven't interrupted us at all." Amelia walked over to the door. "Sir Richard was just telling me some of the fables about the constellations." Chatting amiably, Amelia led the way back to the saloon.

The days and evenings passed pleasantly. The passengers were blessed with fine weather. The few times it rained, there were no heavy winds to toss the ship about. The passengers kept busy exchanging books and devising new games. The adults who were so inclined became instructors to the youngsters. Richard Dyckman and Perry struck up a great friendship; the man had untold resources of patience when it came to answering an imaginative six-year-old's many questions. Amelia watched as they explored the ship, queried the mate, and talked to the sailors. She recognized qualities in the man that would make him a good father and a good husband. But for reasons she refused to recognize, she would not permit herself to see him as *her* husband or Perry's father.

Somewhere deep in her being was the haunting memory of that short, exquisite love affair. Everything that Alfred had offered for her future in devising his plan hinged on that memory. Even though she had agreed that the plan was right and necessary and well thought out, it made no real provision for *her* needs, those needs she had discovered in Justin Farnham's arms.

CHAPTER FOUR

IT WAS APPROACHING eleven in the morning on a fine day in September when the quiet of Princess Gardens erupted with the sound of vehicles entering the square. Neighbors to either side of number fifty-two could have seen, had they deigned to look, the arrival of a magnificent cream-colored traveling coach picked out in gold and black, followed by three vehicles piled high with what appeared to be wrapped furniture, rolled-up carpets, various boxes, parcels, and travel bags. They would also have taken note of the high-stepping horses, the unusual cream-colored stallion with the darker tail and mane, the prancing brown pony, two small Italian greyhounds, and a huge white macaw with a yellow beak that was screaming a greeting to those with the temerity to watch its progress. The parade was being directed by a tall, gray-haired major-domo in cream-colored livery also picked out in gold and black.

The rumor had already gone around the square that the

beautiful lady who was descending from the coach was a wealthy widow, and the little boy was her son. It had also been mentioned that she was a princess—a Russian princess who had been banished from her country because of an illicit love affair with the czar. Or was it that she might be the natural daughter of the late, lamented King of France? Well, whatever she was, the wags said, she *was* mysterious.

Unaware of the conjecture that was flying around the perimeter of Princess Gardens, Amelia descended from the coach and, led by Staunton, entered her abode. She was greeted by a line of servants drawn up in the spacious oval foyer. Her major-domo made the introductions as she paused in front of each one in the line. Once all the names had been mentioned, she thanked the men and women for their work on her behalf and expressed a wish to learn a bit more about them as time went on.

Then there was a flurry of bobs and curtsies and a rustle of starched cloth as the staff took themselves off to their various jobs.

Amelia addressed Staunton. "Let me wander about the house with Annie while you direct the unloading of the wagons. Perry is too excited to sit down and he will want to explore also, so don't bother with us for the while. The place looks lovely; you made a good choice for us." She looked fondly at the servant who was also her tutor and friend. "I can always rely on you, can't I?"

Touched by his mistress's affectionate regard, Staunton responded with a gruff, inarticulate mumble and returned to his tasks.

The foyer was now empty, and the beauty of its black-and-white marble floor was evident. The graceful curved walls and fluted ceiling were painted a pale green. The coved border between wall and ceiling was picked out in the palest shade of mauve, matching the silk mauve and celedon seat covers on the delicate chairs that flanked the Louis XV commodes placed on opposite sides of the foyer. In the curve of the Adams staircase at the far end of the foyer stood a marble-topped table with an enormous arrangement of rubrum lilies and foxglove. Deeply recessed doorways on either side of the entry led to small formal parlors where unknown guests might wait to hear whether or not they were welcome visitors to the household. Beyond the stairwell and to one side was an archway that led to a spacious paneled room. Against the walls were bookshelves holding myriads of worn leather-bound books. The furniture too was worn, comfortable and welcoming. Amelia knew on sight that this would become the heart of the household. There was a kidney-shaped desk where she would be able to attend to her household accounts; near the windows was a large rectangular table where Perry would be able to pile the oddments necessary to his enjoyment of the day's routines; and at the windows were window seats, comfortably cushioned, where both Amelia and Perry would be able to daydream as they watched the changing seasons in the garden.

"Annie, my love," the young widow announced gaily, "I think we are going to be absolutely, perfectly, wonderfully comfortable here. Whatever the rest of the house is like, I shall love it for just this room!" She whirled around, finishing by falling onto the plush velvet-covered sofa. "Let's order tea, then we can go over the housekeeping routine with Mrs. Quince, the housekeeper . . . or do you want to take Perry upstairs to the nursery first?"

"Miss Melly . . . no, I can't call you that any more. I must learn to say Mrs. Carrington." Annie stood stiffly, her hands folded in front of her. "Mrs. Carrington, you can't have tea with me. You're the mistress and I'm your . . . well, maybe Perry's nurse. That's life, and we have to respect the proper way of doing things here in England. It was different in Italy because it wasn't so—so formal as it's going to be here." She raised her hand in the face of Amelia's protestations. "If we don't do things the right way from the beginning, we aren't going to be able to follow Mr. Alfred's plan, and that would be a terrible thing to do to his memory."

"All right, Annie, I understand what you mean even if I don't like it." Amelia looked at her nurse, now Perry's, with her head tilted to one side. "Although how you expect me to treat as a servant a woman who has been like a mother to me is beyond me."

"You'll just have to be an actress, my dearie—like most women. Now, shall I ring for your tea and Mrs. Quince so you can go over the household instructions with her? You'll have to be making up your mind where you want all the things we brought with us."

"Annie, love, do go up to the drawing room and bedrooms and tell them where to put things. You know what I want in my room. Leave everything else until later. I have no idea where I want to place the paintings and bric-a-brac. And I suppose you'd better ring for Mrs. Quince on your way out. When you see Perry, send him to me. I shall feel grateful if I can get some food down him. He's so excited."

A few moments after Annie had left the room, a gentle tapping at the door signaled the arrival of Mrs. Quince. The housekeeper, a short, energetic lady, was attired in a black bombazine gown with the housekeeper's belt and chatelaine at her waist. A flawless white apron covered her skirt and was matched by a lawn mobcap neatly tied under her chin.

"Oh, Mrs. Quince, thank you for coming so quickly." Amelia moved to a straight-backed chair. "Please, won't you sit down? We have a great deal of planning to do, and I think you would be more comfortable."

"Thank you, madam, that's most kind of you." Graciously the lady accepted the appointed chair. "I hope everything is to your satisfaction."

"You have done a marvelous job, Mrs. Quince. I would just like to tell you what I expect and the plans I have for the season. I don't want you to feel that I would surprise you with impossible last-minute demands."

The housekeeper was most appreciative of Amelia's thoughtfulness. "It will be a real pleasure to work for you, madam," she said with a real depth of feeling.

"Well, then," said Amelia with a smile, "let me begin by telling you what I have planned as a start. For the next month we will be very quiet. I must refurbish my wardrobe, and I will be interviewing for a lady's maid and for a tutor for my son. Have you met Peregrine yet, Mrs. Quince?"

"I heard him playing in the garden with his dogs, madam. It did my heart good to hear the laughter of a young'un."

"I've told him he's not to be too much of a bother, but he is accustomed to have the run of the house."

"Don't trouble yourself, Mrs. Carrington. I get along well with little ones. I'm sure he'll be no bother," the house-keeper said comfortably.

"Good, I'm glad you feel that way." Amelia heaved a sigh of relief. "Now, I would like to arrange a series of menus so that we can see something of the chef's abilities. I am planning several dinner parties starting in November, and I shall give a rout after the new year, perhaps in Feb-ruary. Tomorrow we can start to unpack the trunks. The linens will all need washing; they've been packed away for weeks and the sea air may have dampened them." Amelia stopped talking for a moment and paused to think.

"I shall pay a visit to Madame Celeste to start ordering my wardrobe. While I am out, Staunton will see that the paintings and bric-a-brac are unwrapped, and I would like you to see that the porcelains are all washed. I will decide where to display everything later." She stood up, as did Mrs. Quince. "Now, I think I had better find my son. Would you have a nuncheon served to us in my sitting room. Noth-ing elaborate, just filling! I'm so hungry I could eat the wheat sheaves off of the molding!"

As the housekeeper left the room with a laugh, to spread word of Amelia's needs, Amelia climbed the elegant curved stairway to the second floor. She knew, from Staunton's description, that the drawing room and formal dining room were located there as well as her suite of rooms and two other bedrooms.

"Oh, Mama, Mama, come here," she heard Perry's voice calling from the room to the left of the stairway.

"Where are you, Perry?" she called. "Keep talking to me so I can find you before I get lost."

"Oh, Mama, how can you get lost in our very own house? You are very silly!"

Amelia had by now walked through the charming formal dining room without seeing her son. His voice seemed to be coming from behind the baize door, which Amelia made haste to open. A cunning butler's pantry, well lined with shelves and work space, led to the staircase to the lower levels. Standing on a box in front of a chest-high opening was the young master of the household, gazing enraptured into the depths of the dumbwaiter. Actually, he had just climbed off the contraption, having ridden up from the kitchen to this highest level of its works.

"Perry, are you up to mischief already?" his laughing mother exclaimed. "I think we'll have to put bells on you just to make sure we can follow you around. You know, like we belled the cat back home?"

"Oh, Mama, you're always funning me. You can't put bells on people" was the boy's rejoinder.

"My dear child, there is always a first time for everything, so watch your step, sir." Amelia tried to make a stern face at her son, but at his look of skepticism, she burst out laughing. "All right, if you say I can't, I suppose I can't. Instead let's go find my rooms and have our lunch. Mrs. Quince is going to have it sent up for us."

Mother and son gaily set about finding Amelia's suite. They opened two more doors before finding her rooms, which overlooked the extensive garden to the rear of the building, walled in by the stable and carriage house. The parlor was painted the palest green, reflecting the color of Amelia's eyes. The furnishings, though dainty, were comfortable; a chaise longue, a small sofa, and several softly upholstered chairs welcomed the visitors. The russet tones of the fabrics and the pale green of the Savonnerie rug became the perfect complements to Amelia's person. Her tawny hair took on a flamelike color and the translucent quality of her skin was like a priceless porcelain.

Annie was standing beside a small table set for two, arranging platters of delicacies sent up by Mrs. Quince. "It's about time the two of you stopped your rambling and came in for your food. The both of you will set yourselves down for a good rest as soon as ye've finished eating. And don't give me any arguments on the subject either!"

Amelia grabbed Perry's hands and swung him in a circle. "Of course we won't argue with you, Annie, will we, Perry? I'm famished and tired and so happy. Whoever thought we would have such a lovely home. Our Staunton performed a miracle, didn't he?"

"Now, stop your playing and come and sit down. You'll get the child too excited Miss Me—Mrs. Carrington. If you're going to behave in this flibberty-gibbet way, you'll never be taken up by the *ton*. You'll be a ragpicker's lady for sure!" Grumbling, Annie convinced her two charges to sit down for their repast.

"What's a ragpicker's lady, Annie?" Perry wanted to know. "Will I be a ragpicker's boy?"

"Oh, Perry. Now ye see what you've done," Annie demanded. "Yer mother's behavin' like a twelve-year-old." She threw her hands in the air helplessly. "Well, I give up. If I didn't know that you've had nothing to drink from the bottle, I'd say ye were tipsy as a titmouse."

Quickly Amelia began to soothe Annie's exacerbated feelings. She blamed her extraordinary behavior on the heady scent of the roses rising from the garden and the extreme weight of responsibility that was now hers. Her eyes glistened and the tiny dimple at the corner of her mouth came and went as she tried not to smile.

"We shall be good now, I promise you, Annie. After we finish eating, Perry will accompany me to his room and then we shall take a good long rest." Amelia sat down at the table after placing her son in his chair. "You see, we're eating already."

Annie's response was unrepeatable as she tossed her head and busied herself about the room.

When Amelia had returned to her room after seeing Perry to his bed, she directed Annie to fetch Staunton so that they could consider their next step. When Staunton and Annie entered the little parlor, Amelia immediately shared with them her plans for the next few days.

"John, you will have to find the addresses for these people." She handed him a list of names. "I will be writing notes to them to tell them of my arrival and to ask for permission to pay calls. By the time we have settled in a bit more and the first of my new gowns are delivered, we should have received answers and can begin to develop a

social life. Alfred was sure I would be able to get an intro-
duction to Lady Jersey or Lady Sefton through some of
these people. He insisted I must be introduced at Almack's,
although I don't know why, at my age, it's so important to
go to Almack's. It's not as though I were a debutante.''

"If you go to Almack's, it becomes a sign of acceptance
to the rest of society," Staunton said. "Even *I* know that a
lady must be seen by the *ton* in places of the best reputation,
and that is the very best, so don't fight it, Miss Melly. It's
an important step in Mr. Alfred's plan."

"I know, I know. It's just that I sometimes wonder about
that dratted plan. Would it be such a terrible thing if I were
to change my mind about it? I have enough money for two
years at this rate, but suppose I continue like this for a few
months and then, if I meet no one I like well enough, we
could move to the country or something.'' Amelia looked
at her assistants with a plea for understanding. "I might even
speak to Mr. Plimpton about making an investment in the
funds. Maybe we could make the money last even longer
that way."

Shocked sounds came from both Annie and Staunton.
"How can you think of doing anything like that, my dearie?"
"Now, now, you don't want to be hasty, Miss Melly," came
in unison from the two.

"Oh-h, don't sound like that. I know my husband wanted
the best for me and thought I should do my utmost to find
another husband, but what if I don't want another marriage?
What if I don't find a man whom ... I can love?" Amelia's
voice sank to a whisper.

"Oh, now, Miss Melly." Annie reverted to the nursemaid
of Amelia's youth. "You're just a little blue-deviled because
you're so tired. I told you to take a rest. All this traveling
and settling in. It takes its toll of a person. Come along
now. Let me get you settled down for a nice long nap.
You'll feel better for it, and tomorrow you've got those
ladies coming for the interviews, and then you've got to go
to the dressmaker ..."

"Oh, Lord, Annie, don't call Madame Celeste a dressmaker. She's a *modiste*, my dear, a *modiste!*" Bidding

Staunton to return later when he had ascertained the addresses she needed, Amelia laughed wearily as she let Annie conduct her to her bedchamber. "There's so much to do. I wonder if we can get it done," she said to Annie as she sank down on the bed.

Convinced that the young woman would be asleep before the door closed, Annie left the room quietly, after tucking the coverlet around her mistress's shoulders. But Amelia remained awake, thinking of the shadowy, unknown man who might become her next husband. Gradually, as she sank into sleep, the featureless face began to take on the likeness of Justin Farnham. She felt herself running toward him, her feet sinking into a treaclelike substance that slowed her forward motion. The figure she ran toward spread his arms wide; then as she got closer to him, he began to draw back from her. She felt herself calling, "Justin, Justin, I love you. Please, please wait for me . . . don't leave me . . ." The more she struggled to reach her goal, the faster her lover moved away from her. In her dream Amelia began to cry, feeling lost and forsaken. Suddenly the figure of Justin began to grow in size. His face became distorted with rage. "Liar . . . betrayer . . . whore. . . . Where is my son?" Amelia tossed and turned, moaning, "no . . . no . . . forgive me . . . forgive me . . ." until she felt a hand on her shoulder and Annie's voice calling her name.

"Miss Melly, Miss Melly . . . wake up now, do. You're having a nightmare, Miss Melly."

"Oh, Annie . . . I don't know what happened. Such a terrible dream." She brushed her hand across her face and was surprised to find it wet from tears. "I must be overtired, just as you said. Sit with me for a while."

"All right, my honey lamb. Your Annie will stay. Just you rest yourself. Everything will be all right, you'll see." Soothed by Annie's hand stroking her forehead, Amelia finally fell into a dreamless sleep.

CHAPTER FIVE

BY FOUR O'CLOCK the following day, Amelia had made her choice of a dresser from among the four applicants for the position. It had been agreed that the young woman, Mary Kenton, would return on the morrow to take her place in the household. The salary had been set at fifty pounds a year with two summer dresses and two winter dresses to be a part of the annual emolument. In exchange, Kenton would guarantee to keep her new mistress's wardrobe in prime condition, would do minor sewing where necessary, would attend to Amelia's coiffure, retrim her hats, and prepare her for each day's events in the most fashionable manner possible.

The newly hired lady's maid was satisfied with the agreement. She was still young and to have the pleasure of dressing a woman as beautiful as Mrs. Carrington would surely add to her own prestige.

The next day, Amelia, driven by Staunton in her landau, paid her first visit to Madame Celeste's *Établissement de Couture*. With Kenton's approval she had decided to limit her ordering on this day to several morning dresses, two riding habits, a pelisse and a mantua, and one demi-gown and one ball gown. She knew that to become visible to the smart set, without being vulgar, she must be perfection. Her strong personality and character provided her with the manner to become a setter of fashion rather than a follower, so she had chosen to create a wardrobe for herself that would be classic in simplicity of design and cleanness of line. She knew that she had a beautiful body and above-ordinary good looks, and she also knew that she must capitalize on these assets to attract the type of man that her Alfred had predicated in his plan.

Before long Staunton had drawn up in front of the austere white building that housed Madame Celeste's showrooms and workshops. There were no exterior windows to advertise the *modiste*'s wares. Only a discreet brass plaque shining in the sun announced to the world that this was the doorway to that mysterious place of *haute couture*. With a great deal of anticipation, Amelia entered the *sanctum sanctorum* of fashion to be greeted by a tiny white-haired dame dressed in severe black *peau de soir,* relieved only by a white lawn double ruffle around her neck.

"May I help madame?" the woman asked graciously.

"I am Mrs. Carrington," Amelia announced, "and I've come to order a wardrobe from England's most renowned couturière."

"Then you have come to the right place, madame," the petite woman told her. "You are speaking to Celeste. Let us chat for a while about your needs and then I will decide whether I am able to help you." She gestured to the inner room. "If you will seat yourself, we can have some refreshments while we talk. You understand I have a very select clientele and can accept new customers only if their style is such that they will be *à la mode.*"

"I appreciate your frankness, madame." Amelia slowly removed a long tan glove from her right hand. "I would not

consider you as the one person to create my wardrobe if
your standards were not so high." Amelia examined the
modiste's face and saw something there that encouraged her
to confide in the older woman. "I must tell you that I wish
to become *the* setter of fashion in London. I wish to have
a wardrobe of such simplicity that first people will notice
me and then the genius of the designer of the gown. I know
you already have a reputation of being the best in England,
but I wish that upon seeing me in your gowns people will
know you to be the best in Europe." She looked expectantly
at the designer. "Do you understand what I am trying to
say, madame?"

"But of course, Mrs. Carrington. You are blessed with
a beautiful face and a—you will excuse the reference—an
even more beautiful body; but you need my genius to create
the aura of elegance and brilliance you need to . . . perhaps
capture a husband of the *haut ton?*" The little lady looked
at Amelia with a decided twinkle in her eye.

"We understand each other completely, Madame Celeste. I felt I could count on your *savoir-faire.*"

"Oh, yes, already I can see several gowns in my mind's
eye. You must wear green . . . with peridots and diamonds,
and much amber and topaz colors. No pale yellows or blues
or reds, but a plum color might be very nice. A moment
and I shall bring out some fabric samples, and Jeannette and
Clothilde will begin to model some of the day dresses." The
usually urbane woman exhibited an excitement that was
unknown in her shop as she contemplated the creation of
a wardrobe for this unusual Mrs. Carrington. Never before
had a client been so frank. This woman was unique.

Madame Celeste snapped her fingers to summon her
assistant. Quickly she gave orders for a procession of gowns
to be shown to Amelia. With another snap of her fingers
she summoned a young man to carry out the rolls and bolts
of fabrics in the colors she had decided would be best. The
madame and Amelia spent the next hours trying on some
of the partly finished day dresses that Madame had on hand
to see the effect of the style; standing still while Madame
draped and cut and pinned the beginnings of several com-

pletely new designs; and, finally, discussing the proper accessories to go with each gown. On one point Madame was insistent: the ball gown must be of the color and worn with peridots, that exquisite green jewel that has more life and brilliance than emeralds and would reflect the color of Amelia's eyes.

Finally Amelia cried, "I am able to stand here no longer, madame. I shall faint if I try on one more gown. I have already exceeded the number of garments that I was going to order today, which I consider very fortunate since it will cut in half the time I shall have to spend being stuck with pins." The tired young woman laughed. "But it really is very exhilarating to be so successful with one's first order of business. Besides, I find it excessively stimulating to spend so much money!" She ended with a chuckle.

The *modiste* smiled in response to her newest client's elation. "Mrs. Carrington, you will be the leader of the fashionable world before you have time to sneeze! I, Celeste, *je vous assure!* Now let Jeannette help you finish dressing and then have a cup of tea to fortify yourself before you leave my salon."

Gratefully, Amelia let the assistant fasten her dress and redo her hair. The girl exclaimed over the color and weight of the long tawny tresses as she brushed it into the simple chignon that Madame had recommended, leaving a loose, short love curl at each temple. When she had finished and Amelia had signaled her satisfaction, the *midinette* moved to leave the dressing room. Before she left, Amelia thanked her for her services and pressed a coin into the young woman's hand, at the same time asking for assistance in finding the main salon.

Jeannette indicated the direction with profuse thanks, then disappeared to the rear of the shop. As Amelia approached the curtain dividing the passageway from the reception area, she heard Madame Celeste speaking and a woman's voice answering. "Oh, dear, there goes my sit-down and tea" was Amelia's immediate thought as she stepped through the curtain. Once in the room, she beheld Celeste and a rather tall woman dressed in the height of elegance. The woman's back was toward her, but when she saw Celeste's motion to Amelia, she turned to see who was approaching.

"Good Lord, Amelia, is that you?" the woman cried out.

"Eglantine...Eglantine Dalquist...what are you doing here?" Amelia asked in amazement. "What a wonderful thing to see you here."

"Eglantine Winterset now, Amelia. In fact it's the Marchioness of Hexford to be exact. Are you impressed?" The young woman laughed as she spoke, her beautiful smile lighting up a rather plain face. "Where have you been? I haven't seen or heard of you since...since forever."

"Oh, Eglantine, just let me sit a moment and enjoy seeing you again. It's been so long. You look absolutely the last word. Being a marchioness agrees with you, I can tell. When did you marry? Have you children? Will you ever forget the night we stole the bonbons from Lucinda Dalrymple? The whole school was in an uproar! Do you remember?" Amelia's eyes shone with excitement at the sight of her dearest friend from her school days. "Your appearance here is a miracle."

"Well, tell me all, Amelia. Where did you disappear to? I remember you had to leave school because of your father's death, but you never wrote and I couldn't find you. My father tried but it was as if the earth had swallowed you up." Lady Winterset grasped her newly found friend's hand and drew her over to the settee. "Sit down and start talking. I want to know everything about you. Right now!" the marchioness commanded.

Amelia started to laugh. "You were slated to be a member of the aristocracy, Tina. You always had a commanding presence! You can't expect me to tell you *everything* all at once. Madame Celeste would have to keep her shop open for hours and hours. Not really...there isn't that much to tell." Briefly, she related the important events in her life, finishing with "Now I am widowed and the mother of an excessively active six-year-old."

"That still doesn't explain where you've been all these years. Was Alfred Carrington in trade or a lawyer?"

"No, he wasn't anything like that. He was a scholar and a teacher. We used to travel from university to university, where he would occupy the chair of a visiting expert in his field. The last few years we lived in Padua, Italy, where he was honored by the university for his work. But what of you? When did you become a marchioness? Oh, Tina, you haven't changed a bit, except to become excessively smart in your dress! You were such a harum-scarum creature, with a torn sleeve or flounce or your bonnet falling off your head. When did you change?"

"Why, I suppose I grew up at last. Oh, darling Amelia, do you remember how we cried together the first week of school? Why, we were only twelve years old and away from home for the first time. I don't know what I would have done without you. I think you were the only girl who didn't make fun of me for being so plain and having such long legs and arms. Thank heavens the rest of me grew up to match them." The elegant Lady Winterset giggled in a most unladylike way. "And thank the good Lord that George likes long legs and arms. He tells me I'm exceedingly graceful! Did you ever hear such moonshine? That's true love for you! I finished school just before I made my come-out and then met my George the same year. I wouldn't say yes until the next year though. I couldn't believe that such a handsome, divinely top-of-the-trees creature could be in love with me. He was richer than my father, of impeccable origin, and most popular with the ladies. So I finally believed him when he told me he couldn't live without me. And now I have a wonderful husband and two terrible children—a boy and a girl, whom I love madly."

Amelia gazed warmly at her friend. It was such a wonderful feeling to see her joy reciprocated, her friendship accepted and returned. She had never had a friend like Eglantine. One must consider oneself fortunate to have one such friendship in a lifetime.

"I must spend some time with you, Tina. We have so much to talk about. Can you come for a visit tomorrow? Or even later today?" Amelia pleaded.

"Oh, my dear, I would love to come over today. Of all

things that would be the most wonderful. But a friend of George's accompanied me here, and I promised I would go for a drive in the park with him. Let's make it for tomorrow, at half after one. That will give us the whole afternoon together. Have your coachman give the directions to mine." Lady Winterset clasped her friend's hands. "And I do want you to meet this friend. He should be here any moment. You might be just the sort of woman he's been looking for, although I wouldn't be surprised if he never makes a marriage. His standards are impossible to meet." Suddenly Eglantine started to wave. "Here we are, Justin. Come and meet a long-lost friend of mine."

As Amelia heard the name, she lifted her eyes to behold Justin Farnham striding across the room. His green double-breasted superfine tailcoat fit his broad shoulders to perfection, the silver buttons placed so as to outline the tapered wedge of his torso. Tan doeskin pantaloons clung to his well-shaped legs, and his feet were shod in highly polished Hessians, a triumph of the bootmaker's art. The crisp linen of his collar points ended at his jawbone, announcing his moderation in dress. His tie was an intricate salute to his valet's ability and the pale green-and-buff striped waistcoat formed the exclamation point of his costume. His only jewelry was a heavy gold signet ring on his left hand and a single fob hanging from his waistcoat pocket.

Amelia saw a flicker of annoyance cross his face and then a rather formal smile moved his lips, deepening the furrows that bracketed his mouth. Off in the distance she heard the staccato of Tina's voice accompanied by Justin's deep tone. Time seemed to hang motionless as her heart thudded in her ears. She felt a rise of intense emotion that threatened to suffocate her. The sight of his beloved face created an instant response in her body; her skin tingled, her breasts grew taut, her arms longed to hold him. Her face reddened then blanched as the memory of their last encounter replayed in her mind.

"Amelia, what's the matter? You look so pale. Are you all right?" Tina asked.

"I—I . . . it must be the heat and all the standing." Amelia gave a little laugh. "You know it is exceedingly hard work to order a new wardrobe, Tina. I just felt faint for the moment."

Farnham quickly poured some wine from the decanter that had been standing on the table. "Have a sip of this, ma'am. It will make you feel better." He studied the beautiful face of Eglantine's friend as she sipped the wine. "There, I can see your color looking more normal already. Now, if you are up to it, perhaps Lady Winterset will introduce us?"

"Of course, Justin. Don't be impatient. Amelia, I would like to make you acquainted with my friend, Justin Farnham, Earl of Croyville. Justin, this is Amelia Carrington, a dear friend of mine from my school days. And I warn you, scamp, you are not to break her heart!"

"How do you do, sir?" Amelia extended her hand as courtesy demanded. She would rather have run out of the shop and as far away as she could. She had not been prepared for this meeting. It was too soon, too sudden. "Dearest Tina, I must go now. I have so many errands to run. We are newly arrived in town, and I have lists from my cook, my maid, my butler, and my son. I shall expect you tomorrow. My lord, so nice to have met you." As he bowed over her hand, her eyes looked into his for a moment, an endless moment, and then tore themselves away. She forced herself to walk slowly and deliberately out of the room, turning to wave farewell to Eglantine before she stepped quickly through the door.

CHAPTER SIX

JUSTIN FARNHAM FLICKED his whip lightly over his horses' backs. His black high-perch phaeton, drawn by a pair of sleek black horses harnessed in tandem, was the highest kick of fashion.

"Now, tell me about this mysterious friend of yours, Eglantine. Where did she come from? I'm sure I would have seen her before this if she had been making the scene."

Before she started to speak, Eglantine studied Farnham's saturnine face. She had known him for as many years as she had been married, and many times he had proven himself a good friend to her and her husband. But there was a certain recklessness that sometimes seized him, as well as an air of ruthlessness. She knew he could be as gentle as the proverbial lamb. But George had told her stories about Farnham that made her pause before discussing her friend with him.

"You must swear you will not treat her lightly, Justin, before I shall tell you about her. She is not in the ordinary way, you know. She was married very young and was widowed early this year. I don't really know the woman she has become; it is twelve years since we last saw each other. But I loved her dearly when I knew her. She was ever ready for a schoolgirl's romp, yet she also had a depth of compassion and understanding that went far beyond her age. I didn't know it at the time, but looking back now, I well understand the beauty of her character. I remember once when I had played a rather naughty prank on a girl I detested. Amelia knew but suffered a beating from the headmistress rather than disclose my name. At the time, I thought she was the next thing to Joan of Arc. So you must swear you will never do anything to hurt her, Justin. She is not one of your lightskirts."

"You pain me with your doubts of my character, my dear Tina." Farnham thrust out his lower lip in a childlike pout. "You see, you have hurt my feelings and I shall kick my feet and stamp my heels!"

"Oh, don't be ridiculous, Justin. You may tease your lady loves like that, but it won't work with me. I may slap you instead!" Eglantine could not keep from laughing at the sight of the pouting earl.

"It works for your son, so I thought it would work for me." The earl smiled at his companion's strictures. "I would really like to meet your friend again, and I faithfully promise not to seduce her or cause her mental or bodily harm. Now, will you tell me more about her?"

"Justin, really, you're too naughty." Tina slapped his arm. "I can't tell you too much more. She barely had time to say more than what I've already told you. She mentioned that she'd been living abroad for the past six or seven years and that she has a young son. Her husband was Alfred Carrington, the Elizabethan scholar. Did you know him?"

"I heard him speak once at Oxford, but he was twenty or twenty-five years older than I so we were never really in the same social circle. Which must have made him more than thirty years older than your friend Amelia. What kind of marriage could that have been, do you suppose? An age difference like that often leads to horns on the husband while the wife dances merrily around." The earl's handsome face looked cynical. He remembered just such a situation with his own parents. Although the age difference had been less, once the Countess of Croyville had provided her lord with an heir, she never shared his bed again. Her *affaires* had been numerous, and her disinterest in husband and son had left deep scars within Justin.

"You may take my word for it that such a situation would never have existed with Amelia. She's too honorable to have even contemplated being unfaithful to her husband. Once she made a bargain, she would have stuck to it no matter what the effort. That's the kind of person she is, and I'd stake my life on it that she's not changed." Lady Winterset was indignant that Lord Farnham should so misjudge her dearest friend, and she spent the next few minutes in decrying the outspoken earl.

"Pax, pax," he cried finally, with one hand raised and the other carefully holding the reins. "I'm sorry I inferred that your marvel of honesty and trustworthiness was any less than what you have described. However, I would like to meet her again. If you could arrange it, then you could act the chaperone and make sure I do not mistreat her in any way."

"I'll think about it," Eglantine grumbled without promising.

Farnham judged that he had better change the subject; for the remainder of the drive he discoursed on the myths and marriages of the *ton*. He drove the marchioness home but refused her invitation to join her and her husband in a glass of wine while she informed George of the unexpected meeting that day. He drove off as Lady Winterset was being admitted to her home, so he did not see her pause before entering, to cast a long look after him. Eglantine knew from her husband the lengths to which Justin would go to gain his end. She prayed her newly found friend would never learn of his character. But then, why should one meeting disturb her so?

Farnham headed his phaeton for White's. He wasn't interested in placing any bets but thought perhaps he might be able to pick up some word about the mysterious Mrs. Carrington. Surely *someone* at that exclusive club would have heard of her. She was damned beautiful. Not with the usual looks; those green eyes were really an unbelievable color. As he mused, his thoughts turned to Amelia's marriage. What kind of marriage could it have been? He would be willing to bet that she was a lusty wench.

Farnham let his thought dwell on Amelia's form. She certainly had a beautiful shape. A face and figure that could have launched the famous thousand ships. He would give her a chance to settle in and then, through Eglantine or another mutual friend yet to be discovered, he would seek her out. That mouth of hers, those dimples . . . he could almost feel himself kissing her.

While Justin Farnham was letting his thoughts roam over Amelia's person, the young widow was lying on her chaise longue trying to regain her equanimity. The unexpected meeting with the Earl of Croyville that afternoon had come as a shock. She had thought herself prepared to face the father of her child, but she had learned how wrong she had been. That he was acquainted with Eglantine was going to cause a few complications in her life; of that she was sure. She was just as sure—irrationally, she realized—that he had recognized her. Why else had his beautiful mouth curled into that horrible sneer? Well, maybe it wasn't a sneer; maybe it was just a twitch of his lips. No, don't think about his lips, those soft, warm lips that had made her shiver with passion as they had touched her breasts, her thighs, her— No, no don't think about that.

Oh, would it be like this every time she saw him? It was like the attack of some dreadful disease, the fever, the hallucinations. What medicine would she be able to take to make her well? The best medicine would be the man himself, but that would be too dangerous. If he were to learn who she was, the role she had played, he would turn that bright intelligence to her undoing. Who knew what that would mean to her future and especially to Perry's. He might even take Perry away from her. No! He couldn't do that; Perry was Alfred's acknowledged son. But he might tell Perry when the boy was older and then see him turn against her, his own mother.

Amelia! Get hold of yourself! She finally began to gather her wilted edges together. She had been seared by the love for this man who had walked with her down the road of passion to exquisite fulfillment.

The tears that had been seeping from her eyes finally stopped flowing as her breath evened and deepened. She slept for a time, easing her exacerbated emotions.

Soft sounds of movement, the swish of fabric against fabric, gradually penetrated Amelia's slumber. Slowly she raised her eyelids to behold Annie fussing with the brushes, combs, and bottles on the *poudoir*. She watched for a few moments, noting the way Annie would glance at her with a triumphant look, just waiting for Amelia's eyes to open so she could impart some good news to her.

"I'm awake now, Annie. What's giving you the look of a cat that just swallowed the canary?" she finally asked.

"Well, madam . . . Miss Melly . . . we've had a caller. A very fine caller." A bright smile crossed Annie's face.

A pang of fear stabbed at Amelia's insides. He couldn't have come so soon!

"That fine gentleman, Sir Richard Dyckman, has been and left his card. He expressed to Staunton his hope that you were well settled in and that you would not be too tired to give him a few minutes of your time on the morrow. And them's his words exactly!" Annie leaned back against the dressing table and brought her hands together in a exultant clap.

"Why, it was very courteous of the gentleman to pay a call on us. His manner certainly leaves nothing to be desired, and when he calls again I shall probably see him. But Annie"—Amelia's voice took on a warning note—"don't get any ideas in your head. He's not the man for me."

Amelia turned away from Annie's perceptive look. She couldn't share her fears with the dear nurse yet. Oh, if only she could just meet Justin and pretend she had never known him before. If only they could start afresh. But she felt it could not be. There was too much deceit and secrecy on her part. He would never forgive her imposture, and she was not so sure, right now, that she could forgive herself.

CHAPTER SEVEN

TISSUE PAPER AND boxes were heaped on the floor and on the chairs. Bonnets, shoes, scarves, and gloves were still lying about. Kenton was doing up the last tiny pearl button at the back of a wine-colored mull day dress with *point d'esprit* sleeves of a paler shade. The *point d'esprit* bodice insert was topped with a tiny ruching from which Amelia's slender neck and beautifully shaped head rose like a flower on its stem. The tiny ruching was repeated at each wrist, accenting the fragility of the graceful hands. Velvet bands shaped the gown to her ribs just below the breast and were repeated above the fashionable ankle-length hemline.

"Madam, you look ravishin'." Kenton stepped back to examine her mistress. "The color makes your skin look like that rice porcelain."

Amelia joined her maid in laughter. She had recovered

from the megrims the sight of Justin Farnham had brought on and was once more enjoying life. She had occupied herself in sending cards to Alfred's many friends to reintroduce herself and in entertaining the few friends she had made on board ship. Captain Englander had paid her a morning call just three days previous and Signor and Signora Pacelli had attended her one afternoon.

Today Richard Dyckman was to pay her a call and take her for a drive in his curricle. He had stopped by twice since that disastrous day at Madame Celeste's, and the house was abloom with the flowers that had arrived from him every day since she had taken up residence in London, two weeks ago. Today she would have to find the words to convey to Sir Richard her appreciation for his friendship without encouraging him in his pursuit of her hand. She liked him too much to accept the offer she knew he wished to make. It wouldn't be fair. Better that she remain unwed. Perry's inheritance combined with her jointure would be enough to allow them to live simply. The boy was young enough to learn to enjoy country life unadorned by the trappings her marriage to wealth might bring. Now that she had decided to follow her own destiny, whatever it might be, she didn't have to rush into anything.

Kenton finished smoothing the hair that had become untidy, then pinned the dainty lace and mull cap in place on Amelia's smoothly coiffed head. "It's such a shame to have to cover your lovely hair," she said as she worked, "but it surely does look well on you. Most ladies add ten years to their age when they wear their caps, but you look ten years younger."

"Why, I thank you, Kenton, for your kind words and your very effective way with a comb and brush. Shall I cut my hair, do you think? I'm getting rather tired of this style." Amelia looked at herself in the mirror with a questioning air.

"Oh, no, madam, everyone wears their hair in a frizz and it's become so common. Your hair is so smooth and glossy. It's much more elegant. And the two little curls keep it within the fashion without looking like all the other ladies." Kenton offered a soft bee's-wing cashmere shawl to her mistress. "You fairly make me proud to call myself your dresser. You have a *look*, and that's special!"

Pleased by her maid's praise, Amelia arranged the soft shawl about her shoulders as she left the room. It wasn't quite time for Sir Richard's arrival; she would be able to spend a few minutes in the study going over her household accounts. The bills from Madame Celeste would be presented soon along with those from the bootmaker, milliner, furrier, and all those others from whom she had been buying merchandise as though she were rich as Croesus himself.

Amelia was just finishing the addition on the last of the bills before her when Staunton entered to announce Sir Richard's arrival. She rose quickly and followed her major-domo into the green salon, where the nobleman was awaiting her presence.

"Dear Sir Richard," she greeted him with her hands outstretched. "It's turned out to be a beautiful day for a drive. I'm so glad you invited me to accompany you. How have you been? Your flowers are lovely. Such an extravagance, but so welcome."

The tall, well-dressed man held Amelia's hands for a moment, bestowing a look of great tenderness upon her. "Mrs. Carrington, as ever lovely. You outshine the sun today. I'm forever grateful that the flowers pleased you. You make it very easy to do such things for you."

"Now, now ... such flattery! You shall turn my head completely around so that nothing will please me. You set such a high standard for others to follow." Amelia refused to become serious or to accept Sir Richard's comments as more than pleasantries. She was not yet ready to turn him off. He was a good friend, and she would miss his company if he were to take his attention away. Yet she did not want him as a husband. "If you would give me just a moment to put on my pelisse, we'll be able to go for that drive."

Ruefully Dyckman nodded in agreement. He had never yet met a woman who had so attracted him; nor one who was so immune to his approach. Although she was everything polite and charming, she refused absolutely to hear him when he made an advance. She accepted his tenderings as the merest flattery of a skilled man about town.

Perhaps after she had been in town for a month or two she would be more ready to listen to him. The diplomat's thoughts turned to the December holiday season. It might be possible to arrange a country party over Christmas. His mother had been after him to spend the time with her at Abbot's Combe. She would be thrilled if he were to suggest entertaining friends, especially if he mentioned that he was considering marriage. Lady Dyckman had been trying to marry him off for years. He, of course, had not felt a wife a necessity. His relationship with Mrs. Stanford had satisfied his occasional need for the more carthy pleasures, but now that he was going to be offered an ambassadorship, a wife such as Amelia could be a decided asset.

"Sir Richard, you are far from this world. What can you have been thinking of that I've had to call your name these three times?" An amused Amelia finally broke into his thoughts. "Are you solving the problems of the world? Or just of England?"

"No, just thinking of my mother. I had a letter from her today complaining of being lonely in the country." Amelia's escort held the door for her as he spoke. "Of course she had no fewer than five guests staying with her at the time, she wrote, but that, to her, is an almost empty house. She considers a day without the arrival of new faces a day lost in boredom!"

Staunton held the great front door open for them as they left the house. Sir Richard's curricle was at the curb, his horses held by his groom. The baronet lifted Amelia onto the seat, then jumped up beside her. He directed his groom to return to Princess Gardens in one hour and then lightly touched the backs of the glossy brown horses with his whip.

Amelia lifted her face to let the sun touch her cheeks under the large poke of her bonnet. Her green eyes shimmered with pleasure at the crisp October air, the scent of the fallen leaves, and the brilliant color of the trees and shrubs. A few late-blooming flowers could be seen in the central gardens where some walkers were enjoying the weather. The horses moved through the light traffic at a brisk pace, the metal on their harness and bridles jingling softly as they trotted down the avenue. The driver and his passenger carried on an intermittent conversation about the weather, the season, the persons they passed; they were enough at ease with each other not to have to fill each moment with speech. As they whirled into St. James Park, they were forced to slow down by the congestion of landaus, carriages, curricles, and phaetons dawdling along, their passengers doing their utmost to see and be seen.

"I believe half the *on-dits* are thought up along this avenue," Amelia commented as she watched the passing parade. "You can see, just by the expressions on the faces, who is telling a delicious story and who is telling one too scandalous to be spoken aloud! Why is it so necessary that the English *ton* be such gossipmongers?"

Sir Richard laughed gently at Amelia's reading of the scene before them. "My dear Mrs. Carrington, I think you will find the same behavior in Paris or Rome or Vienna— anywhere in the world where you have a wealthy, bored, purposeless society. People who are busy living their lives productively have no time for the stories these people take joy in bandying about. I suppose society such as this needs to pull its members apart so that those who do the pulling can feel more acceptable to themselves by contrast."

"It's truly sad to see it," Amelia responded. "I had forgotten—in fact had never really experienced—this scurrying about looking for activities to occupy empty time. I've always seemed to be busy in my life. Alfred and I lived such a different life. Thanks to his being accepted in university circles, our contacts were with people who, for the most part, found great meaning and worth in the lives they led. Rather than gossip about the living, it was their greatest joy to try to unearth gossip about the long dead!" She hurried to expand her statement at Sir Richard's shout of laughter. "You know what I mean, now stop laughing! The emphasis was on understanding the minds of the great thinkers in order to better understand their creations, whether it was art or music or literature or science. I found it to be most exhilarating. I wonder if I shall be able to comport myself with the empty headedness that seems to be expected of the women of the *ton*."

"Do you mean to proclaim yourself a bluestocking?" asked Sir Richard, gasping with laughter. "You, with your beauty and manner, could probably carry it off. People will speak of you as being an *original*, which might not be such a bad thing. That way you would set your own style—say what you wish to say, go where you wish to go, read what you wish to read, see those whom you wish to see. Have you the strength of will to carry it off?"

"An original? Shall I have to be brought into fashion, do you think, or can I carry it off on my own?" Amelia was intrigued by the possibility of circumventing the expected polite and rather shallow behavior of the *ton*.

"I think you could do it with the help of a dear friend of mine. Let me introduce you to him, and then you can take his advice as to how to go on."

"Who is your friend? I am quaking in my boots at the thought of meeting someone you obviously consider terribly influential." There was a decided gleam of mischief in Amelia's eyes. "Shall I behave in a saintly way or in the manner of a sinner?"

"Mrs. Carrington, stop cutting me the wheedle. If my friend likes you—and I have no doubt that he will—you will be made without having to raise your little finger. If he takes you in dislike . . . well, I wouldn't care to think about that." Dyckman looked down at her with a corresponding gleam in his eye. "Just so that you will continue to quake in your boots, I shall tell you that you are going to meet that nonpareil, the best of the best, Beau Brummel! Are you quite properly impressed?"

Amelia clasped her hands together in mock supplication. "Oh, please, sir, I shall be good. Don't, I pray you, suffer me such a punishment. I promise never, never to get out of line again." She was no longer able to stifle her laughter and let it out free and hearty—and most unladylike, said the looks that were cast her way by some of the passing throng.

A member of the parade gazed at her from half-closed eyes. Seated atop his restive gray stallion, he was partly hidden by the overhanging branches of the tree under which he had stopped. Justin Farnham watched the play of expressions that crossed Amelia's face. In repose her beauty had a serenity and stillness that made one wish to penetrate the mystery of her being; in activity her face had a vivacity, an animation that called to one to join this adventure, this exploration of the wonder of living. Without being aware that he had signaled his horse to move forward, Farnham found himself closing in on the lively scene he was watching. Bemused by the widow's mobile features, the earl was soon in view of the curricle. As Amelia turned from Dyckman to straighten her skirts she became aware of Farnham's intent regard. Her instinctive response was to draw back from it, but there was no place to remove to. Her face paled as her eyes were caught by the deep gaze of his black eyes. Her limbs felt weak and a glimmer of thought gave thanks that she was seated. Finally Farnham broke the palpable tension by lifting his hat in greeting and moving to the side of the curricle.

"Mrs. Carrington, I believe we were introduced by Lady Winterset. You seem to be enjoying the day. Sir Richard, nice to see you again." The earl's words were courteous, and his cold good looks were softened by a small smile of greeting. His lordship was rather puzzled by the drastically altered Mrs. Carrington. Moments before she had been sparkling with laughter and now, only since he had greeted her, she had become quieter and more formal. Putting the change down to a reserved demeanor or a European formality, the earl continued to chat for a few moments.

Trying to maintain her composure in the face of this unexpected encounter, Amelia found herself studying this man who was the father of her child. She noticed that his face had a more finely drawn look to it; perhaps the indentations, like parentheses, on either side of his mouth were deeper. And his mouth . . . As her eyes traced the outline of the molded lips, she could feel their caress . . . the softness as they had taken little love nips down her neck and across her breasts. A shiver swept through her body and called Sir Richard's attention to her.

"You must be cold, Mrs. Carrington. The weather seems to be changing," he commented solicitously. "Will you excuse us, my lord, I'm afraid the lady will take a chill through my negligence. I must see her home." Casually touching his hat in a salute to the earl, Dyckman lifted the reins to signal the horses to move on.

Farnham watched the curricle, his thoughts taken up with Mrs. Carrington. She interested him greatly—there was a sense of familiarity when he looked at her but he was sure he had never met her. According to Eglantine, she had never been in London before, and yet...and yet...He must see her again.

She would be a superb playmate, of that he had no doubt, but beyond that he wanted no entanglement. Just once had he been ready to offer his heart to a woman, only to lose her without warning. No, these feelings had nothing to do with his lost lady Mystère. Why had she left him so suddenly, without a word?

The earl touched his horse with his crop, moving on along the path.

CHAPTER EIGHT

"PERRY, PERRY, ARE you ready?" Amelia swept into her son's room. She discovered him dressed for riding, head down in a huge packing case, his legs moving in an effort to keep him from tumbling in. "What on earth are you doing, child? The horses are at the door, and Staunton has been standing with them these last fifteen minutes."

"I can't find my crop. I can't go riding without my crop. What if Captain won't gallop? Please, Mama, help me find it." The child's head emerged from the trunk so that he could turn the full effect of his pleading eyes on his mother.

Amelia laughed at the boy's expression and bent over the box to help him. It was amazing, she thought, how like his father he was, even to the look on his face when he wanted something. They must never be seen together. "Here, Perry, here's your crop. Now let's go for our ride.

58

I'm bursting with energy and need you to look out for me! You shall be my ... guardian, and watch that no highwaymen come after me!"

"Oh, Mama, you say such silly things. Are there *really* highwaymen in the park?" The youngster's imagination began to work as the desirability of meeting up with a highwayman became apparent to him. "Do you think I could save you? Of course I could. I'd hit him with my crop. Slash, whop! And then charge Captain straight at his horse, hallooo!"

"I think I've unleashed a monster," Amelia murmured to herself. "Now he'll be fighting highwaymen for the rest of the week!"

Mother and son were soon mounted, Amelia on her cream-colored horse and Perry on his pony. Amelia dismissed Staunton, assuring the major-domo that she wouldn't need him this early in the morning. There wouldn't be enough traffic to worry about the streets, and the park was sure to be empty of all but the most intrepid riders. Sitting straight-backed on their mounts, the child and the woman set off for the park. Amelia occasionally bent her head to answer Perry's many questions about the area through which they were passing. Her severely designed deep-green velvet riding habit served to enhance her femininity. Her hair, the color of a lion's mane, was worn tied back with a ribbon in the way of men of an earlier year. It hung down her back, golden against the dark color of her habit.

Amelia pointed to the right. "There, Perry, we have to go down that street to go to the park. Move to the side of the road. There's a bit more traffic here than I thought there would be. Be careful, darling. Some of the drivers are rather careless." Amelia moved her mount so that she was between Perry and the oncoming vehicles. "It's hard to believe it's October; it's such a perfect day. Have a care, Perry!"

"Oh, Mama, I can do it all right. See, Captain is very good and goes just where I want him to." As he rode, Perry turned his head to speak to his mother. Unknowingly, as he turned he pulled on the left rein, forcing his little horse to move into the lane of traffic. A rapidly moving phaeton came a hairsbreadth too close to the frisky pony. The rush of air as the wheels almost brushed the animal's legs was enough to set the horse in flight. Suddenly it took off toward the park at a speed that it had never before attained. Startled, Perry dropped his reins and was unable to catch them again. He leaned forward and grabbed the pony's mane with both hands and hung on for dear life.

Before Amelia was able to kick her horse into following, the wildly swaying phaeton lurched to a halt between her and her runaway son. In the moment or two it took for her to get around the offending driver and his phaeton, the pony was halfway to the park entrance. She let out her reins and urged her great horse on, calling out to Perry to hang on.

Suddenly she saw a horseman, riding like the wind, veer after the boy into the park; the pounding of the flying hooves repeated the pounding of her heart. The horseman caught up with the pony and was able to lean over and take the reins, slowly drawing both his and Perry's animals to a halt.

As Amelia rode up, with eyes only for her son, she heard the boy exclaim, "Oh, that was capital! I was hardly afraid at all. Did you see me, Mama? I think I was very brave not to fall off, don't you?"

"Oh, Perry, thank God you were so brave." The young mother laughed as tears fell unheeded down her cheeks. She reached out to touch her son as though to check the reality of his condition, then extended her hand to his rescuer, whose identity she had missed until this moment. She looked up into eyes of the same glowing sable brown as her son's.

"I say, Mrs. Carrington, are you all right?" the Earl of Croyville asked Amelia as she swayed in her saddle.

"Yes . . . no . . . I . . ." She brushed her gloved hand across her forehead, letting it rest for a moment on her temple. "I just felt faint for the moment. Thank God you were here, sir. Perry," she called to her happily burbling son, "make your 'thank you' to Lord Croyville. If it hadn't been for his quick action, my dear, you might have been badly hurt."

Protesting that he had been fine and it had been a capital adventure, Perry expressed his gratitude to the earl, then resumed his direction down the riding path as though nothing had happened.

"Shall we play follow-the-leader, Mrs. Carrington? Your son seems to have taken charge and expects us, his troops, to follow along behind him." A droll smile lightened the earl's features, reminding Amelia once again of the charming man she had known those years ago.

Unable to resist his smile and indebted to him for her son's safety, Amelia guided her horse alongside Farnham's. She rode without speaking, in a quandary as to how to conduct a casual conversation with this man she had known so intimately. It was difficult enough to try to keep her senses. She would have liked to have fallen into his arms without further ado. As she thought of the results of such an action, her cheeks became stained with a rosy hue. Much aware of her blush, she gave the earl a sidelong glance to see if he were observing her. To her chagrin, he was openly watching her face, his smile no longer apparent but with a slight crease between his brows—almost as though he were puzzled by her appearance.

"Have we met before, madam?" He asked the question slowly, as if in doubt of his own senses.

"Oh, no, I'm sure I would remember if I had met you previously, my lord. Why, I've only recently returned to England after a rather long absence. And before that I lived a very quiet life with my husband. He was a literary man, you see, and much involved with university life. No, I'm sure we've never met before." Amelia babbled like a brook. She realized that her response to his question was too extreme and quickly excused her manner on the grounds that she was still upset by Perry's accident. Then, hoping to turn his thoughts from her, she began to chat about the current social scene. "Are you going to Almack's for the opening festivities, my lord? I understand everyone will be there."

"I hadn't planned on it. I've been to too many of the openings over the years. Why, had you planned on going?"

"Well, I've never been, you know. Eglantine—Lady Winterset—called yesterday and insisted that I should make an appearance. She is quite friendly with the Countess Lieven and says that she will have no problem getting me a voucher." Amelia paused for a moment, looking thoughtful. "I'm not sure that I would care for the activity. I *am* a widow and don't really desire to be sitting on the sidelines with the dowagers and chaperones. It's rather an appalling idea, rather like a horse fair, I should think—all the young debutantes being examined by all the young, and not so young, eligible men!" Her eyes gleamed with amusement. "I should imagine *you* would like it very well, being a man, but I don't think *I* should like it quite as well, being a woman!"

The earl let out a peal of laughter. "I've heard it described as many things, madam, but not as a horse fair. It's considered to be a most respectable place, the finest marriage mart in all of Europe. Well, England anyway! I do promise you this, though. If you should decide to accept Eglantine's invitation, you will not be left to sit among the dowagers. In fact, I herewith engage you for two waltzes and a stroll at the intermission. Shall we say the first and third waltz?"

Amelia's eyes tangled with the earl's as she looked at him in astonishment. A long, speechless conversation took place in which questions were asked and answered and statements were made that left both parties breathless. The earl's lips twitched in the semblance of a smile as Amelia, with difficulty, suggested that she would have to think about accepting his invitation to the dance. "After all," she said breathlessly, "I'm not even sure I shall be going."

"What, shall you cry craven? Surely you are as brave as your son." The earl's cheeks were deeply creased in a broad smile. His eyes dared her to take him up on his challenge.

Her chin held high, Amelia replied, "I should be happy to dance two waltzes with you, sir, if, by the time you arrive at the ball, I have any dances left. Perhaps the stroll would be too much. We don't want people to start talking when it's all a hum anyway!" A smile lit the earl's dark face in appreciation of Amelia's answering challenge.

"It will be necessary for me to attend you before any one else can, won't it, madam? D'you know, I can't get over the feeling that we've met before. Yet I can't remember where or when."

"Perhaps it's just that I remind you of someone. I've frequently been told that my face has a quality that makes it reminiscent of many others." Amelia struggled to quell the terror she felt that her secret would be discovered. She knew she must be bold, that if she showed the least sign of uncertainty, he would know.

The two fell silent. The onslaught of the intense response she was undergoing, combined with the fright she had suffered when Perry's pony ran away with him, left Amelia exhausted. At the same time there was a tingle of exhilaration running through her veins. The challenge of renewing her relationship with Farnham could not be called boring. It was a dangerous game, but like a fruit that is forbidden, it was the more delicious in the eating. If he should discover their former liaison, if he should awake to the fact that she was his "masked lady," he might be so rabid with anger as to denounce her to the polite world. She must keep up her pretense, and try with all her might to disengage his interest in her; for it was obvious he was interested. She had no doubt this interest was more for dalliance than the honorable estate of marriage. After all, she was well born but not of the highest level of society, as was the earl. And he had seemed to have made it obvious that he was not the marrying kind, else certainly he would have found himself in a parson's mousetrap long since.

While Amelia was racking her brain for a way to avoid adding to the earl's knowledge of herself, he was trying to catch at the wisp of recognition that was buzzing around in his head. When she smiled, that was when he most felt that he knew her. It was the dimple, flickering in and out. But who did it remind him of? Someone he had not seen in a long while, that was certain. Perhaps a childhood memory. Surely he would have recognized this woman with her extraordinary beauty and those incredible green eyes had he met her before. Deciding at last that the day was too short to waste in unproductive thought, the earl resumed his bantering conversation with his companion.

"Have you made plans to view the exhibition at the British Museum? Lord Elgin's marbles remain one of the wonders of the earth, according to some accredited viewers."

"I had not really thought to make the effort. Having lived

with the wonders of antiquity abounding around me while in Italy, I find that there is no novelty in seeing more. I brought back two or three pieces of small sculpture, one of Etruscan work. It has a very mysterious quality to it. To be honest, I prefer paintings to sculpture. Color and life as expressed by the artist give one a refreshing interpretation of that which may be worn out from one's own point of view. Don't you agree?"

For the next several minutes the earl and the widow chatted about their mutual likes and dislikes as well as their disagreements concerning art and literature. Occasionally they were interrupted by Perry, who would canter back to them to inform them of a most wonderful object or person or animal he had seen in his investigation of the park precinct. Each time he received their comments and then left them; afterward they would be silenced for a while, caught in their own thoughts about the singular effect each was having on the other. Then they would resume their conversation, rarely becoming personal, although Farnham tried his best to learn more about Mrs. Carrington's past. He couldn't imagine that she had been contentedly married from the time she was seventeen to a man so much older than she. Surely, he thought, she must have indulged herself in a liaison or two. She appeared to be much too sophisticated to have been content to remain the virtuous country wife.

Amelia, sensing his cynicism, was sincere in her answers to everything but that short two-week period seven years ago. All her feelings toward this man were being rekindled, and she appreciated the danger he represented to Alfred's plan. She could almost succumb to him if he were to offer her *carte blanche* ... almost!

Their talk turned to the subject of current fashions and some of the extremes to which the so-called arbiters of fashion were willing to go to achieve their uniqueness. Commenting on the padding and corsets that some men wore, as well as the exceedingly high collars, Amelia added that she knew the earl detested the scratch of stiffly starched points against his cheeks because of the tenderness of his skin.

"But how would you know that, Mrs. Carrington?" was the question the earl posed in a slightly surprised voice.

"Know what, my lord?" Amelia realized she had made a *faux pas*. There was no way she should have known whether or not his skin was that delicate. After all, men were supposed to be rugged creatures.

"About my skin, of course."

"But don't all men have delicate skin on their cheekbones? My husband was very chafed about the face. I naturally supposed you would have the same inclination, because I thought all men had the same problem." She was able to utter the words with the greatest of surprise, all the while thinking that she never appreciated her abilities as an actress so much. Well, not since the lady in the mask had existed.

"Oh, yes, of course." Farnham accepted this reason. "I almost forgot your husband."

Amelia began to question the earl about his family and friends, asking about likes and dislikes and habits, pretending to compare them with her husband's. When she exclaimed artlessly to have just realized that all men were not as alike as she had thought them to be, the earl was forced to laugh. He decided that this woman was really an amazing person. Her knowledge of art and literature and the general aspects of society as a whole were very advanced for a woman, while her knowledge of men and women and the *haut ton* was very naïve. Curiously delightful to have both aspects in one woman, especially one as attractive as this. The earl's pulse beat no slower than did Amelia's when he thought of the delightful dalliance he could enjoy with her if his wooing were successful. Her naïveté might slow her understanding of his goal, but she was not stupid. She would become aware of his objective sooner or later. For now, it did not matter if it were later. The machinations to achieve his ends were proving to be very enjoyable; and a pleasure delayed would be a pleasure more deeply enjoyed for the waiting!

As if Amelia sensed the gist of Farnham's thoughts and had to change the subject, she began to speak of ending the

ride. "We've been out for too long already. Oh, not that
your company made the ride tedious, my lord. But truly I
have guests expected this afternoon and Perry must rest."
She turned her horse as she spoke and gestured to Perry to
join her.

"No need to say good-bye just yet," the earl said. "I
wouldn't dream of letting you return home without accompanying you. Traffic is much heavier since we arrived in
the park. I shouldn't wish to have to ride to the rescue again!
I think if we leave the park at the West Road, we'll find
it a bit easier to get to Princess Gardens."

The spate of traffic as they rode towards the Carrington
residence precluded any conversation. When they arrived
at number fifty-two, she directed Perry to take the pony to
the stable and to send a groom to fetch her horse.

Farnham had dismounted to help her from her animal.
Holding Amelia in his arms for an instant as she slid down
from the saddle, his strong hands gripped her waist so that
her toes were just above the walk. He held her so that her
eyes were on a level with his, her breasts resting against his
chest. She could feel his heartbeat like an echo of hers, and
there was the merest trace of a flush on his high cheekbones.
She held herself as still as a rabbit being hunted in the field;
her wish was to fling her arms around him and lose herself
in his kiss. She saw her wish repeated in his gleaming eyes.
Before he could take advantage of the position in which he
held her, she turned her head to look down as though searching for a foothold. She began to express her thanks for his
help, refusing to meet his eyes again.

With great reluctance the earl allowed her to slide down
until her feet were on the ground. Then with great élan, he
lifted her hand and brought it to his lips, carefully placing
a kiss on the inner side of her wrist.

"May I call on you, madam? The day after tomorrow?
Perhaps you would join me in a drive?" His eyes challenged
Amelia, a challenge she couldn't bring herself to accept but
was not quite ready to refuse.

"I don't know whether it will be convenient, my lord.
The duties of a mother..."

"I think I deserve that much reward, Mrs. Carrington, for saving your son's life."

Was he really grinning at her? Amelia lifted her chin. "Very well, my lord, if you insist. Carringtons always pay their debts." She gave a little chuckle. "Two o'clock, day after tomorrow?"

"That will be perfect. I look forward to seeing you then. Please give my good-byes to your son. He's a delightful little fellow." Farnham waited until Amelia had entered the house before remounting his horse and taking his leave. If he had realized the extent of the turmoil he had produced in the young woman's breast, he might have extended his stay to take advantage of her weakening resolve.

CHAPTER NINE

"GOOD GOD, JUSTIN, that's the ninth neckcloth you've spoiled tonight. Is this your usual practice?" David Hollings, Justin Farnham's friend, laughed. "Is this the scamp who was more often covered with mud than covered with clean clothes? Where, oh where, are the joys of yesteryear?"

"Enough, wretch. You perceive before you one of the wonders of English manhood. So envied, so emulated, so exalted that nine neckcloths are as nothing to achieve the look known as the Farnham fall." The Earl of Croyville postured with hand on hip, gesturing with his quizzing glass. "If you insist that we go to White's tonight, then I must look up to the mark even if it means twenty cloths!"

"Oh, what monster have I unleashed?" moaned Hollings. "Please, friend, can you not pretend to perfection? None will say you nay."

"If you will promise to make my apologies to the Beau, should he notice, I will accept whatever happens to the next tie, *sans peur et sans reproche.*" Farnham took a sip from his glass of wine, then gestured to his valet for a fresh piece of linen. "If I wrap it thus, and tie it so, and then bend my head v-e-e-ry slowly to let my chin rest on the material in this way, *voilà,* we have it . . . that desired Farnham fall. Do you like it?"

"If it looked any different than any of the other nine, I might be better able to give you a true answer. Cawker. Your admirers should see you act the clown. Why do you play this kind of a game, Justin? Are you so bored? I thought you were beginning to look on the married estate with more favor now that you've met the lovely Mrs. Carrington." Hollings joined arms with Farnham as they walked out of the dressing room. "Don't look at me as though you'd like me to shut up. Everyone is talking about the two of you. How long has it been? Just short of three weeks and already you've been seen driving or riding with her six times. That's the first time you've set out after a respectable woman in longer than I can remember."

"Has it been that often? Of course sometimes we met by chance. I've really only seen her by appointment twice." Farnham was silent as they descended the stairs. "I cannot deny that she is a very beautiful and most charming woman. She has wit and warmth, a rare combination. But she is not so different from most women, I imagine. Once the novelty of knowing her wears off, she would probably be just as much an encumbrance as all the others. I prefer short involvements with no obligations to the unbearably taxing situation of a marriage." The two men entered the dining room.

"Well, if you're not interested in her, I may just take up after her myself. I doubt she's the type to accept a *carte blanche,* even from you, my friend." Hollings whisked the tails of his jacket out of the way as he sat down to the dinner table. "The truth is, I may put you out of the running altogether. I have decided that the time has come for me to consider the honorable estate of marriage. In fact, my father has threatened to disown me if I don't bring home a bride within the next six months. He claims he won't be able to rest happily unless I provide him with a grandchild before he goes. Just to make sure of the succession, you see. The old humbug, he would like to have a dozen grandchildren to whom he could teach all his tricks."

"And shall you be sure to oblige him, David?" The earl waved aside the dish being proffered him by a footman. "Try some of the *ragoût*; the cook has proved quite adept at the seasonings. Why are you so particularly interested in Mrs. Carrington?"

"For the obvious reasons—youth, beauty, brains, fortune. She strikes me as being a woman who would be infinitely various in her attitudes. And it intrigues me to be your rival!" Hollings leaned back in his chair as he spoke. "It puzzles me that she should appear from nowhere, as it were. Where did she come from? Where is her family? And who was her defunct husband?"

The earl thought a moment before speaking. "You know her story. She married as a veritable child, too young to have made her come-out. And you know her husband, or knew him, just as I did. I think of a sleeping princess when I think about her. There is a liveliness of nature under her quiet demeanor." Farnham glanced at Hollings. "It's strange, David. I keep having the feeling that I've known her. There is something about her that seems so familiar, yet I can't place her."

"Perhaps she reminds you of someone from your youth."

"That's what she suggested. Said she'd been told before she had the kind of looks that reminded people of others they had known. But that's not it. I feel as though she was very important in my life. Strange . . . I can't seem to get over that sense. It's actually very annoying. Wish I could shake it."

"Why not try seeing her more often by arrangement? You've seen her at Almack's; the two of you were very noticeable when you waltzed together. Perhaps you should try to attend her more frequently at the more formal affairs." Hollings seemed concerned about the earl's impression.

"Didn't we have an invitation for Lady Wilmot's ball tonight? Ever since Brummel was so kind as to notice Mrs. Carrington, she's been seen at all the best functions. She's absolutely sure to be at the Wilmots'. We're dressed for it, no need to change. Spend a half hour or so there and then we can go on to White's or wherever. Perhaps seeing her with other people will help you recall where or who or what your memories are about."

"Dear fellow," responded the earl, "you know I don't enjoy these big crushes. I've avoided them as much as possible these many years past. However, I think you've made a good suggestion. I should like to see more of her more often." The earl began to laugh. "I feel like one of those elderly gossips who function as chaperones, gossiping away about a perfectly blameless lady. Are you finished with your dinner? You'd better take another sup of wine. You won't get any worth drinking at Wilmot's; he keeps the worst cellar I know of. . . . Let's go, let's go. You've piqued my curiosity now, and I won't be able to rest until it's satisfied."

The earl turned to his butler to ask the time; upon learning that it was not yet nine o'clock, he suggested to his friend that they withdraw to the library and enjoy a cigar before leaving for the evening's entertainment. He refused to spend any more time discussing Mrs. Carrington and instead led the talk into a discussion of the latest news from India.

The two men spent a leisurely hour over brandy and cigars, then called for their cloaks and left for the Wilmots' ball.

As Farnham and his friend were discussing Mrs. Carrington, a parallel discussion was occurring in Eglantine Winterset's dressing room between Tina and Amelia. Amelia, escorted by Sir Richard Dyckman, had dined with Lord and Lady Winterset and was engaged to continue on to Lady Wilmot's with them. As the two women were refreshing their hairdos and shaking out their skirts, Lady Winterset was giving her opinion of Amelia's escort.

"He's a very nice man, Amelia, but a little quiet, don't

you think? I think his being a diplomat for so many years must have made him so. Can you imagine trying to have a fight with someone in the diplomatic corps? Always uttering the most devastating words in the politest of manners. Really, Amelia, I should want to hit him with a poker!" Lady Winterset pantomimed a crashing blow with a weapon of enormous size. "I hope you don't betroth yourself to anyone before you have had a chance to meet all the eligibles."

"Tina, you're incorrigible." Amelia warded off her friend with a laugh. "I am quite able to make up my own mind on many subjects, dearest. And I certainly don't intend to make so important a decision as marrying before I am sure I know the one I wish to engage very well indeed. Richard is very sweet. In many ways he reminds me of Alfred, but I don't want that kind of marriage again. I'm not sure he would be the right father for Perry. The child is so bright and active, always asking questions and wishing to be going about. Richard has patience, but even now, when he wishes to please me, he cannot really give the time to the boy. His career is forever taking him to one place and another." Amelia looked at her friend. "I don't want to be on the move, at least not with him. He's a good friend to me, Tina, and that's all he'll ever be." She paused a moment, hesitant to say what she really meant: I want to marry for love, if I marry at all. And to someone closer to my own age, but for love.

"Well, it's too soon to be adamant about any decisions. Don't eliminate Sir Richard as a possible choice, my dear. He could offer you much in the way of money and position. You would never have to worry for the future, and life is much better for a married woman than for a widow."

Eglantine leaned toward the mirror to adjust her earrings. "Have you met anyone you are interested in? Besides Justin Farnham?"

"What do you mean, besides Justin Farnham? I'm not interested in him, not a bit." Amelia turned her back to Eglantine and busied herself with her fan.

"Naturally not. I knew I was mistaken. It is for the very reason that you are *not* interested in him that you turn pink when his name is mentioned, is it not? Or that you turn white when you see him enter a room. Certainly you show very decidedly that you are not in the least interested in him." Lady Winterset adjusted the drape of her demi-train.

"Well, if I show any interest, it is because he reminds me of someone I had a great concern for many years ago." Amelia smoothed her hair and tried to show a lack of regard for the subject matter of the conversation.

"Of course that would be the reason, I had not thought of that." Lady Winterset abruptly changed the subject. "Shall you be going to the benefit for Kean next week? They say he is to do both Shakespeare and something from the 'Comedia Del Arte' plays. Such a talented man, but such a terrible temper, I have heard."

Amelia, grateful for the turn of the conversation, began to chat about the events offered by the London theaters. Her answers were rather absentminded until Eglantine once again mentioned Justin Farnham.

"Who do you think would make a better husband, Sir Richard or Justin? If I weren't so happy with George, I might set up a flirt with Lord Croyville. I have a feeling 'twould be *most* exciting. But I do love George to distraction, so that takes care of that!" Lady Winterset laughed at her own fantasy.

"How can you talk so, Tina? Even if you were not happy with your husband, would you really have an *illicit* affair? I know it's thought the thing to do. Marriage is looked upon as a convenient closet in which to hide one's *outré* behavior. But for women like us? It confuses me: to contemplate marrying and then looking outside of the marriage for the excitement and satisfaction that so many women tell me they find in their little affairs." Amelia sat down on the edge of the chaise, more interested in talking with Eglantine now that such an interesting subject had arisen than in joining her waiting escort. "I've often wondered, Tina, is it . . . normal for a woman to feel enjoyment in the . . . um . . . you know. . . ." Her voice faded as her face turned fiery red. "Oh, why is it so difficult to speak of the subject even though we are two women?"

Eglantine took pity on her embarrassed friend. "My dear

Amelia, you were married for twelve years. Do you mean to tell me that you never spoke of the physical side of marriage with your husband? Surely as an older, more experienced man he took the time to tell you and teach you?"

"Well, he was kindness itself, but we didn't have too much . . . that is, he was ill for some time and . . . oh, it was all done very quietly . . . not like . . ." Amelia's hand covered her mouth before she said anything else.

"Not like what, Amelia? Did *you* have an affair? With whom? A gorgeously handsome Italian nobleman, I'll warrant. I never would have thought it of you. Tell me, tell me *all!*" The marchioness sat down next to her friend, ready to coax every last detail from her unwilling lips.

"Please, Tina, don't badger me. It's something no one knows about and I'm not about to tell anyone, not even you. It was something I had to do, although I must have been mad, but it was really for Alfred's sake." Amelia covered her hot cheeks with her hands, too confused by the sudden disclosure of her indiscretion to be able to think clearly. "I will talk to you about how I feel now, but I promise you I won't talk about that time. I have no one of my own age to speak with, so please forgive me if I go beyond the limits of decency."

The woman who was one of the leaders of London's *ton* nodded her head, looking at Amelia with a mixture of affection and puzzlement. She had always considered her beyond the enticements of the flesh, although with her fiery nature she was no further removed from it than anyone else. "You may trust me, Amelia. I love you, you know, and I owe you for more than one beating you took in my place. Ask me anything. I will try to be honest with you and tell you whatever I know."

Slowly, hesitantly, Amelia began to speak of her marriage with Alfred, of how gentle he had been and how undemanding of his rights as husband. She had found the experience in his bed to be occasionally pleasant but never exciting. He was her husband and will she, nil she, it was her duty and obligation to allow him to have his way with her whenever he chose to exercise his rights.

"I was so grateful to him, and really loved him as friend

and father and husband. It was not a hardship, you understand, Tina. It was something one did. I would compose recipes sometimes or plan the next day's activities, and soon he would be finished and we would go to sleep. We went along like that for . . . oh . . . for several years, and I kept hoping that we would have a child, but it never happened. I had been to see doctors and had spoken to experts, but no one could give me any hope. Some thought it was my fault and some told me Alfred's seed was weak, and that we would probably never have a child. Then he went to Italy, and I was to follow once he had made arrangements for a home and such things. Oh, you will think me a wanton when I tell you, and truly, it happened more as a sacrifice to my fondness and gratitude for Alfred. At least it started that way." Amelia stopped to compose herself.

"What started what way?" the impatient Eglantine asked.

"I decided to have an affair."

"An affair . . . but with whom?"

"It didn't matter with whom as long as he fulfilled certain requirements of a physical and mental nature." Amelia's voice was almost a whisper.

"Amelia, I shall choke you if you don't speak up and tell me this story."

Bravely Amelia threw back her head and spoke defiantly. "I decided to try to have a child by another man."

"You decided to have a child by another man! You mean Perry is *not* Alfred's son? I can't believe what I'm hearing." Tina dropped back against the cushions of the chaise.

"He is Alfred's son in every way except . . . that. Alfred loved him, adored him, and cared for him. He was all that could be wished for in a father, but he was more a grandfather. When he realized he was dying, he decided I must find someone who would be able to give Perry the same care and attention he had given. You must never, never say anything about this to anyone, *ever*, Eglantine." The tears began to well from the sad green eyes gazing at the marchioness. "I didn't do it for my own enjoyment. I did it to have a child to give Alfred. He wanted one so badly, and I really wanted to please him."

Tina put her arm around Amelia's shoulders. "Amelia,

if this is too difficult, perhaps you would rather speak of it some other time. We do have two anxious escorts awaiting us."

"No, now that I've started, I must speak or I feel I will go mad. Things are happening, feelings in my body that I don't understand." Amelia drew a deep breath and composed herself before she continued with her story. "I looked over the men who were in town that season. I was not making the *ton* scene, but I read the pamphlets and papers and spoke to some of our friends who were more on the *qui vive*. From a distance, as it were, I studied various gentlemen for their looks, their deportment, their achievements, and their reputation amongst the women, and when I finally settled on a man, I set myself up to seduce him."

"You what!"

"You heard me correctly. I decided to seduce him. But I also knew that he must never know who his seducer was, which I felt would not be important to the one I chose because he was forever with other women. He had a reputation as a womanizer, but with flair." A wan smile crossed Mrs. Carrington's face. She continued: "I was successful in my endeavor. He never knew who I was and never saw my face. I wore a mask for all our encounters and spoke with a French accent. I don't think he would ever recognize me just by seeing me."

"I'm glad for that. It could be quite troublesome to have a former lover come up to you in the street, tip his hat, and say 'Shall we meet again, madam?'"

"That's not the problem; the problem was and is, I found that my body did things that I never knew it was capable of. He—he made me cry out with pleasure, Eglantine. I felt so lewd, so lascivious. I always thought such feelings were for loose women, bits of muslin. Ladies were not supposed to respond with such vigor, and now I don't know. I could never speak of it to Alfred, although sometimes I'm not so sure he didn't know because there was a difference to our bedding. He was a little more . . . interested. I'm afraid Eglantine, afraid that I am really a loose woman because I find that I have met someone who awakens those feelings in me, and I don't know what to do about it. I cannot have a . . . just a . . . I have to be very careful because I have Perry to look after.

"I didn't tell you the worst part of the whole story. I fell in love with my lover. His mind, his wit, his whole self were so exciting to me, not just the time we spent together in a carnal way. Oh, God, I am so ashamed, but in every way he was wonderful. So I ran from him before I shamed myself and my husband by giving myself to him forever and losing whatever place I held in society." Tears were dropping slowly down Amelia's petal-smooth cheek.

"You must calm down, Amelia, my dear. I can't answer your questions as long as you're crying; you won't hear a word." Lady Winterset held her friend in her arms and patted her back. She realized that, despite her age and her experience with a husband and a lover, Amelia was as innocent in thought as a babe.

"There, I'm glad to see you've used up all your tears for the moment." Gently Eglantine wiped away the damp tracks on Amelia's face. "Now, you freshen up your face and I will tell you all I know about men and women, which *I* know thanks to an understanding husband." Gently, matter-of-factly, Lady Winterset led her friend to a new understanding of herself. Amelia found it reassuring to know that she was not a "lost" soul just because she had enjoyed her liaison with Justin. In fact, she was one of the fortunate ones to have this added dimension of pleasure. She learned that it was normal for her to have a physical response, and that she was not to feel ashamed of her body. Undoubtedly, the many months, in fact years, since she had enjoyed her wifely pleasures made her bodily demands understandable. It was nature's way of recalling to her the duty she owed to her race, for what was the product of a loving relationship between man and woman but the propagation of the species.

Feeling like a girl, Amelia was suddenly shy with the worldly Lady Winterset. "I appreciate your understanding, Tina," she said. "I've been going mad trying to get along with all these feelings that I'm having lately. I feel much more . . . *dégagé* . . . with myself now."

"You know, Amelia, I think it only fair, now that I've been such a help to you, that you tell me the rest of your story." Tina looked at Amelia with level eyes, quite serious in manner.

"The rest of the story? Whatever do you mean?" Amelia refused to meet Tina's eyes.

"My dear, it's an open book to me that you are much taken with Justin Farnham, and he with you. He's called on you several times since he met you. Is he the one? Is he Perry's father?"

"Eglantine, never, never repeat that. Justin was my lover but he doesn't know, and I cannot tell him. He'd hate me forever if he knew how I had used him. I am aware of his pride, and I think that no matter how he might feel about me, no matter the depth of his love—if he loves me—he would be implacable in his disgust should he learn the truth." Amelia's voice was vehement, then it softened and took on a dreamy quality. "It would be true happiness if I could live the rest of my life with him. I love him so much that I am truly in pain from it. But I fear his knowing. I have been giving consideration to Sir Richard as a husband. I imagine he will be making an offer. I know he would take care of me even though I have said I would rather not have a life of moving about. Still, beggars cannot be choosers, can they?" Her lips twisted in a wry smile. "I seem to turn like a weather vane, don't I, veering whichever way the wind blows."

"I don't understand what the problem is. You need not tell Justin about your previous encounter. Just let things happen in the natural course of events. He need never know."

"Ah, but he would know, once we were intimate. There is a mark, a birthmark shaped almost like a heart on my body. He would recognize it, for there could not be such another mark exactly alike. No, I think I shall have to give up my love for Justin. It's a luxury I can not afford."

"Amelia, if Justin really loves you, he will forgive you. It's just a matter of telling him in the right way, at the right time. He is truly most smitten with you, and he is, despite his reputation, a most understanding person. He has been a very good friend to George and to me, although, of course, there has never been anything that I can recall that would have had the same effect on him as this." Eglantine's head lowered in thought. "He has all the qualities that you have described as necessary to your happiness, including love. Certainly he is worth taking a chance for. Be patient. Once he has succumbed totally to your charms, he will be most anxious to have you with him always. Don't do anything hasty about Sir Richard. He is a very pleasant man but not, I think, for you."

"I hope you're right, Tina. God knows my heart cries out to this man." Amelia's head dropped into her hands. "Not only my heart, but my mind, my senses. . . . Oh, I hope you're right."

Reassuringly patting Amelia's shoulder, Eglantine said, "I am sure I am. Come now, we've been up here for an age. It's a good thing my darling George thinks all women take forever to primp, but Richard may not be as understanding. Do you feel any better?" She looked a question at Amelia. "Shall you be all right for the rest of the evening?"

"Oh, darling Eglantine, my best of all friends, I feel blooming, like a daffodil in springtime!"

Suddenly life had a new sparkle for Amelia. Her dearest friend had assured her that all would be well, and she chose to believe it.

CHAPTER TEN

THE HUGE CHANDELIERS sent glittering reflections down upon the precisely moving dancers executing figures of the Sir Roger de Coverly. The blacks, dark blues, and deep maroons of the men's formal jackets gave brilliance to the many hues and tints of the ladies' gowns. Feathers, flowers, and jewels adorned the heads, necklines, and shoulders of the carefully coiffed, bescented females. Those not dancing—the chaperones, the elderly, and the wallflowers—sat on stiff white and gilt chairs observing the courting habits of the *ton*. Here and there were small eddies of courtiers attending the worship of one of the incomparables, the belles of the ball—those fortunate young women with the outstanding looks and fortunes who attracted the eligible males and their counterparts, the fortune hunters. The sprightly music offered a counterpoint accompaniment to the soft sounds of speech and laughter and the fall of dancing feet.

At the entrance to the ballroom the lean, dark-visaged Earl of Croyville was engaged in conversation with the Countess Bermot and Lady Wilmot. He was attended by his friend David Hollings, who had evidently said something amusing enough to call for a brief titter of laughter from the countess. As the music for the dance ended, Farnham excused himself from further speech with the two ladies and made his way across the room. He had been watching Amelia's progress during the dance just ended, and now went to claim her for the waltz about to begin.

"You promised me this waltz, Mrs. Carrington" were his only words as his eyes marked the exquisite beauty of his partner. Her dress, of the shade of green associated with spring, was of a perfect design for her figure. The wide, square-necked, low-cut bodice outlined her firm round breasts, exposing just the beginning curve of the creamy white skin. The deep-green lace inserts that defined the high waistline were repeated at the edge of the tiny smooth sleeves that barely cupped her shoulders. Around her neck and in her ears were jewels of peridot and diamonds, rivaling her eyes in color and brilliance. Honey-colored hair, dressed in the Spanish style and adorned with a jeweled comb, capped a regally held head that dipped slightly in acknowledgment of the earl's reminder.

Her gloved hand accepted the arm clad in midnight-blue superfine; her green eyes were captured by her escort's dark-brown gaze. The touch of his hand at her waist as he guided her to a position appropriate to the performance of the waltz seemed to sear her skin through the layers of organza and satin of her gown. He shifted her hand from his arm to the high arching position resting in his grasp required by the dance and waited for the music to begin. There was a palpable tension between the two, remarked upon by the more astute of the assembly to whom the earl was known and the lady was a mystery. It was also remarked upon that, other than the opening phrase uttered by the earl, not a word had been spoken by either party as they took their places on the floor. Slowly, almost casually, the earl of Croyville began to move to the music, guiding his partner in a slow, swooping figure, his hand at the back of her waist firm and masterful. Her body moved without thought, satisfied to let her lover take the lead. Time was suspended; vision was confined to the eyes of the partner. The population of the ballroom became a blur of colors; the sounds faded until only the dance itself became the motivating force.

What words, what vows were exchanged in the speechless language of their eyes? In Farnham, a rising tide of need filled his thoughts. This woman seemed to be the embodiment of all he had ever desired in a female. Her form, her face, her fathomless regard served to enflame his senses ever more.

Amelia let herself respond to the signals her body was receiving from Justin. The quivering flame that raced through her loins, that enveloped her senses, mesmerized her. She became like a leaf blowing in the wind of Justin's desire, willing to, nay bewitched into, forgetting her objections to such an alliance. Enraptured by the thought of resuming the liaison she had run away from many years ago, she was almost mindless in the earl's arms. In truth, she was not even aware of herself as aught but the instrument of Farnham's pleasure and thus her own.

The endless moment of the dance came to its finish. Still speechless, Justin led Amelia to the side of the room, slowly walking with her, still caught in the enchantment of her presence. As experienced a man as he was, Justin was unaware of anything other than desire for Amelia. To his conscious mind she was the prey and he the hunter. He refused to accept his appreciation for her wit, her manner, her companionship; she was food for his fulfillment and nothing more.

Amelia, on the other hand, bemused as she was, knew that she loved him with a love that was beyond anything she had ever known. So much so that she was willing to compromise herself. Willing even to believe Eglantine when she had told her it was worth taking a chance to know that love. If she could not have him one way, she would have him another, even if it meant jeopardizing Perry's future.

And if she could not keep him, once he learned the truth, then she wanted no one. There would be nothing to savor in a life without Justin, she realized now. Her body was aflame; her heart palpitated tumultuously. She prayed that her agitation was not apparent to her companion.

As the thoughts whirled round in her mind, Amelia absently greeted one or another of the few people she was acquainted with. Her arm was still captive to Farnham's grasp; he could not bear the thought of being out of contact with her for a moment. The next set formed, drawing away those people who might have remained to comment on the earl's unusual behavior. Aware that they were, for the moment, free from observers, Justin guided Amelia to the staircase leading to the entry foyer.

"I must speak with you alone," he murmured in her ear. "It's impossible here. Let me call for my carriage and take you home. The evening is almost over anyway."

"I can't. Sir Richard will wonder what happened." Amelia whispered, her eyes huge as she stared at Justin.

"I—I'll come back and tell him you had a headache. You were unable to find him and asked me to conduct you back to your house." Justin paused for a moment in thought. "In fact, I'll leave a message for him with the lackey. He can give it to Dyckman as soon as we leave."

"I shouldn't . . . it's not right!"

"It's necessary. I must be with you alone. We have to— please." Before Amelia could answer, Justin requested his carriage from the footman. In the few minutes it took for the vehicle to be brought round, he instructed another to seek out Sir Richard Dyckman and convey to him Mrs. Carrington's regrets; she was ill and had to be taken home. She would speak to him on the morrow.

Amelia watched the earl as he ordered his troops about like a general preparing for battle. She shivered at the thought that she would be alone with him in a short while. She wanted nothing more than to be in his arms. Her need for the fierce strength that was his was overwhelming. Before she was able to question her actions, the earl had taken her cloak from the footman and wrapped her in it. He supported her out to the carriage and half lifted her into it. As she sank back against the pale-gray velvet squabs, he directed the coachman to Princess Gardens, telling him to take a turn around the park before arriving at that address.

Suddenly, almost without movement, he was on the seat beside her, clasping her hands in his. In the light from the torches outside the carriage, her face was pale, her eyes dark and frightened. She heard him mutter what sounded almost like a prayer and then felt herself drawn into his arms with a vehemence that left her helpless. "Oh, God!" he said as he lifted her chin and met her lips with his in a passionate kiss. Her breath seemed to leave her body when she felt his touch. The hard pressure of his mouth filled her with an ecstasy that made her memories mere shadows. His hands moved from her face as he enfolded her in his arms. She reciprocated by slowly putting her arms about his neck, then pulling him to her and clinging with all her strength. Breathless from her kiss, Justin finally lifted his head to gaze deeply into her eyes.

"I've been wanting to do that all evening. If you hadn't come with me, I think I would have kissed you in front of the whole world." He began to place delicate little kisses along her jawbone and down to the hollow of her neck. "God, I want you. You're the most beautiful thing I've ever seen. Amelia . . . Amelia!"

"Justin, you must stop. . . ." Amelia found it difficult to speak. She'd been breathing with difficulty since Justin had taken her in his arms. "This is madness! I . . . Oh, God, I love you. No, you mustn't." She pushed his hand away as he began to pay homage to her breast. "Stop. I can't let you take me like a . . . a . . . whore . . . here in the carriage. What are you thinking of? Please, Justin, stop." The excess of emotion finally produced tears and deep, rending sobs.

Justin responded as though he had been dashed with ice water. "Forgive me, Amelia. I didn't mean to frighten you like this. I seem to have lost my head. I'm not always so impatient that I must attack a desirable woman in my carriage." Gently, the earl disengaged himself from the distraught woman, holding her loosely around the shoulder as he calmed her exacerbated feelings. "There, there . . . don't cry anymore. I just want to make you happy." Softly he kissed her eyelids, lightly licking away the lingering teardrops. "Very salty, for one so sweet." He laughed wryly. "That's the first time my kisses sent anyone into hysterics!"

"It wasn't your kisses that made me cry. I frightened myself because of my . . . the way I felt. I have never had this kind of feeling with anyone else, Justin—not even my husband." Amelia could feel the blush stealing over her cheeks. "I think you are too dangerous for me to know. For, in truth, I don't know whether I could deny you your goal another time, my lord."

The earl was somewhat taken aback by Amelia's honesty. She was a most unusual woman. He couldn't decide whether she was playing an especially deep game, or if she was actually as naïve as she represented herself. Could one who had been married for so many years and to a man so much older than she . . . it was possible, he supposed, for Amelia to have been a virtuous woman, but his aim now was to have her give up that virtue. She would enjoy life so much more if she were to free herself from such old-fashioned thoughts. And she would make *his* life so much more enjoyable, of that he was sure. Her response to his kiss had given him an inkling of the passionate nature she hid under that serene exterior. He could play her game, and win at it!

"Don't deny me your presence, Amelia. I am beginning to find it necessary to my continued happiness." The earl placed a kiss in his companion's trembling hand. "Say you will allow me your company, my sweet, and I shall promise to guard my behavior—unless you command it otherwise," he murmured *sotto voce*. "I am truly enamored of you, and shall certainly fall into a decline if I am refused admittance to your favor!"

The earl ended his plea with a laugh, finding that he really meant his words but was unable to accept his already-made commitment to this woman. He was afraid of giving up his independance, of coming to rely too closely on another person for his happiness. He'd relied on his Mystère years before, only to have her disappear without a word. Never again would he allow himself to be so vulnerable. The pain was too great. Now, though he was face to face with the one person who could make his life heaven by sharing his future with him, he refused to acknowledge that his feelings were more than lustful.

The carriage slowed to a halt as he was talking. "I think we've arrived *chez* Carrington," he said. "Let me help you into the house and see you settled with your butler. We must continue the tale about your headache even with your servants; it's been my experience that the servants spread more gossip than the masters. So watch your tongue."

Amelia descended from the carriage as though in a dream. She felt emptied of all feeling, though at the same time she wanted only Justin's continued presence. In truth, she was so pale as a result of their encounter, she looked ill. When Justin saw her face by the light of the now-opened door to her home, he felt a stab of guilt for having reduced her to this pass.

"Let me come in with you. No, no, I shall not do anything out of the ordinary," he said in response to her pleading look. "I want to make sure you have a restorative before I leave you."

The earl directed Staunton to fetch some brandy and glasses to the library as the major-domo divested him of his cape. Placing his arm lightly around Amelia's waist to lend her support, he guided her to the quiet, book-lined room. Before he sat her on the sofa, he felt her lean back against him, resting her body against his for a moment. He tightened his arms around her, touching his lips to the top of her head; it fulfilled a tenderness in him that he had never known. For a short interval he wished to truly take care of this woman, to hold her and protect her from such as himself, almost as one might feel toward the woman one wished to marry. Silently he laughed at himself, believing his response was a result of his desire for Amelia as his lover combined with his tiredness at the end of a long day.

"Here, my dear, drink some of this." Justin poured a glass of the brandy that Staunton brought in. "It will relax you and ease your sleep tonight." He watched her as she sipped the liquor, wincing at the biting taste. "I am going to leave, but not before you agree to see me in the morning. I shall take you driving so that no one will think our being together this evening was anything out of the ordinary. I am told that the *ton* has come to expect to see you with me on my morning drive. You don't wish to stop now, do you?" The dark eyes questioned the green that were drooping with weariness. When Amelia nodded, too tired to speak, Justin bent to place a light kiss on her mouth. "I won't ask anything more of you, just the drive tomorrow. Go to bed now and don't think any further of our ride home."

Amelia sat on after Justin left the room. She was in a mild state of shock produced by the unexpected events of the evening. Her emotions were mixed. One moment she felt grateful to Justin for having removed her from the crowd at the Wilmots'. She could not have continued to behave correctly after that dreamy, lovely waltz that had so undone her. And she was angry that he should take such advantage of the disordered state of her mind produced by the dance. She had no longer any doubt that he was a libertine. His behavior in the carriage proved that. But she loved him desperately. A tear slowly made its way down her cheek. What to do? What to do? Her tongue stretched out to the side of her mouth to catch the teardrop. It really was salty, just as he had said. How strange, to lick the tears from her eyelids . . . and how provocative. Obviously, he knew tricks that she would never in a thousand, thousand years think of. It was too much to think on any more. Better to sleep and see what happened tomorrow.

Amelia started for the door. Before she had a chance to open it, it was opened by Staunton. "Madam, Sir Richard Dyckman wishes a word with you. He is concerned that you are ill and would like to assure himself that you are being properly cared for." Staunton frowned. "Shall I show him in?"

"Sir Richard . . . oh, I had forgotten. Yes, Staunton, show him in. If he was so concerned as to come here, I should show my appreciation by seeing him in spite of the hour." Amelia resumed her seat.

Sir Richard's face showed relief at seeing the young

woman seated in the chair. "I beg your forgiveness for arriving like this, but when the message from Lord Croyville reached me, I was naturally very worried. Lady Winterset and her husband expressed surprise that you were not able to personally speak with them, so I took it upon myself to see you and give them a report as to your health." Amelia had the grace to blush at the implied accusation of unpardonable behavior. The baronet continued; "Have you the headache still? Have you taken a remedy for it?"

"I am so sorry to have disrupted your evening, Richard. I had just finished dancing with Lord Croyville when I was overtaken with a weakness and then my head started to ache abominably. There was no time to advise anyone of my malady, so Lord Croyville called for his carriage and brought me home." Amelia held out her hand to the disturbed man. "Please tell me you forgive me . . . friend. I have had some brandy and will have Annie give me a few drops of laudanum when she puts me to bed. You will excuse me now, won't you? Perhaps you would come for tea tomorrow afternoon. I shall be right as a rivet by then. The excitement of the ball . . . too much . . . and I'm so tired now."

Sir Richard could not question Amelia's look of *distrait*, but something suggested to him that this was not the result of a simple headache. He dropped to his knee at her side, taking her hand in his. "You know," he said, "I would like to help you. I know how difficult it can be for a woman alone, even a woman of means such as yourself. I have become very fond of you, Amelia. But I will not speak of that now. I want you to know that you can count on me when or if you ever have a need for help. When you are fully rested and recovered from all this excitement, we can speak more on the subject. Just know that you are always in my thoughts."

Amelia looked at the kneeling man. She knew he was ready to offer her an honorable marriage and that he would take care of her and Perry to the best of his ability. He had a gentleness of character and a strength that she would find herself able to lean on. But was it enough? Could she live without the excitement that she felt in Justin's presence? She had been told many times that in any marriage one partner loved the other more; that it was better when the man loved the woman with a greater intensity, as Alfred had loved her. But now, now that she recognized her love for Justin, she knew that would never again do for her. Somewhere in life there must be someone who would love her with the same passion, someone who could share with her so that she wouldn't yearn over him and he wouldn't yearn over her. There would be an equality and a quality to their love. For now, if it was necessary that she love with the greater fervor, then so be it. She could not live without the love she felt for the earl.

CHAPTER ELEVEN

"KENTON, IS MY violet wool kerseymere dress pressed? I think I shall wear that this morning. No, the neckline doesn't fit properly. It must be sent back to Celeste. The brown with the pale-beige embroidery on the hem, and the matching pelisse. Oh, hurry, hurry. I must be ready when he arrives." Amelia was behaving with less than her usual cool detachment this morning. Kenton rushed around the room trying to help her mistress gather together the clothes she wished to wear, putting away the disgarded garments, and wondering to herself what had caused Mrs. Carrington to behave so.

"Madam," she finally said, "I beg you to sit down and compose yourself. I shall never get your hair done or finish dressing you if you continue to run around like a chicken without its head!" The dresser clapped her hand over her mouth and turned scarlet. "Oh, madam, I'm so sorry. I never meant to call you a chicken. Oh, please forgive me...."

Amelia had stopped her aimless movements, struck by the maid's description. Suddenly she burst into laughter. "You were right, you know. I feel better for laughing, and do forgive you. I think you have more fogiving to do than I, Kenton. How could I expect you to do your job with me running around as you described?" She moved to the *poudoir* and sat down in front of it. "Here, now you can do my hair and then I shall finish putting on my dress. I just want to look my very best this morning." She halted her confidence before she betrayed herself to her servant. "It's so beautiful and . . . and . . ." Her voice slid into silence.

Any day that Justin took her driving or riding was a beautiful day. He made her come to life in a way she had never known, not even when they had their short-lived affair. As Kenton carefully wound the coils of the heavy, honey-colored hair into a chignon, Amelia hugged herself, relishing each moment of awareness of herself.

Last night had been a breach of the earl's normal behavior, it was true, but today she would see that they did not go beyond the boundaries of proper behavior. It had been the waltz. She understood now the objections offered to that dance; it truly enflamed the senses. Indeed, good sense fled altogether in such a state of exaltation.

Definitely it was Justin's presence that lent such a rapturous import to the event. The feeling of his firm hand on her waist led to the memory of the interlude in his carriage. She felt that same astonishment that his touch seemed to produce in her. His kisses had been urgent, ungentle, evoking in her body the feelings that she had been so ashamed of when she had spoken to Eglantine. Now she could relish them—now that she knew she was not unnatural in her appetites.

Abruptly, Amelia was once more impatient to be with the earl. Her dreamy state underwent a change, and again she was rushing around attempting to put the finishing touches to her attire. Kenton threw up her hands in disbelief; there seemed to be no reasoning with her lady today.

While Amelia was giving Kenton fits and starts, Justin

had arrived at 52 Princess Gardens in his elegant high-perch phaeton. Standing at attention on the step at the back of the dashing conveyance was a young lad dressed in the striped lavender and black of the earl's crest. The tiger jumped down from his perch and ran to the head of the first horse of the tandem.

"I shouldn't be too long, Septimus. If it's above five minutes, walk them for a bit. And when I take the reins again, I shan't require your presence. You may return home until I send for you." Farnham finished his instructions and ran lightly up the steps of the portico. Impatiently, he used the knocker, tapping his foot while he awaited the opening of the door.

As he raised his hand to repeat his summons, the door opened and Staunton's apologetic face appeared. "My lord, sorry to have kept you waiting. Our macaw escaped from its cage and Master Perry required my help in capturing the bird." The butler led the nobleman into the foyer and relieved him of his tan beaver hat as he spoke. "Madam will be with you in a moment, sir. If you would care to await her in the blue room. Would you care for some coffee or chocolate? Or something stronger?"

The earl declined with thanks, too impatient to sit and drink coffee while he anticipated his coming encounter with Amelia. His feelings were mixed after the passionate interlude of the preceding evening. True, it had been of exceedingly short duration, within an ace of not having happened at all; but what it had done to him was indescribable. He must have this woman, all fire that she was. She had been frightened by his ardor last night; he must go more slowly, win her confidence before he attempted to seduce her. He had given the question of marriage with her a token thought but decided against it; their relationship was going to be too passionate. Such excessive feeling was not for those who tied the knot. That bond needed cooler heads, a more businesslike approach.

As he contemplated the delights of a loving association with Amelia, the earl heard her footsteps approaching on the polished marble floor. A sudden increase in his pulse surprised him; he had not thought himself so vulnerable to her presence. He knew, of course, that she affected his susceptibility in an acute way, but this was extraordinary. Only once before had he had this kind of turbulence. He had almost lost his heart that time, but never again. He must remain in control of himself and his situation. But it was more pleasant, in a way, to feel this excitement!

The earl paced the room restlessly, waiting for Amelia to make her appearance. When she finally came through the door, he was as surprised as if he hadn't expected her at all. Her tawny hair was partially covered with a small-brimmed deep-brown velvet hat that sat on the back of her head and gave her a look of childlike innocence. A small yellow rosebud wrapped in a sprig of feathery fern was pinned to the collar of her pelisse, which was buttoned demurely to her chin. The cut and fit of the coat belied the innocence of her hat, draped as it was to the outline of her body. The earl took in the young woman's appearance with a quick glance. His eyes rested on her face, drinking in her beauty, examining the lips that had given him so much pleasure in their brief encounter with his.

Amelia greeted the earl with a bright smile, feeling as if her heart might burst. From under lowered lashes she examined the man who had so taken her fancy: his broad shoulders were clothed in a deep russet broadcloth jacket of a doublebreasted style. A paler rust-and-cream striped fabric made his waistcoat, and his strong thighs were clothed in pantaloons of pale beige. On his feet were high white-topped boots. His striped cravat was tied *à la Bergami* over moderately high collar points. A small ruffle cuffed his wrists under the sleeves of his jacket, the softness of the lawn in sharp contrast to the large, shapely hands.

"My lord, you have picked a perfect day for a drive. It could almost be late spring instead of late autumn. Shall we leave now? I am ready, as you see." Amelia had extended her hand to the earl as she greeted him, not quite prepared for the lingering kiss he placed on her wrist. His soft, cool lips sent a shock of excitement up her arm, causing her hand to tremble in his. For a long moment her eyes met his, sending messages of her love to him.

"I see you are looking radiant as the day," he responded

softly, allowing his glance to admire her without responding to her message. "Your man mentioned that a macaw escaped from its cage. Do you run a menagerie here? I've heard the sound of dogs and the chittering of some other kind of animal when I've waited your coming at other times. Who takes care of all your pets?" Justin was impelled to chat about inconsequentials; he was fighting a forceful desire to tell Amelia of his amorous feelings. At the same time that he felt in control of the situation and could coolly plan Amelia's capitulation to his charms, he felt like a schoolboy caught in his first encounter with puppy love.

"Yes, we do have a collection of sorts. They're my son's. He refused to leave Italy without all his pets. Fortunately, we were able to dissuade him from bringing his garden snake. It was a bitter disappointment when the snake hastened to depart from the box in which he was kept and never had the graciousness to return to wish Perry farewell. The poor boy had great difficulty in accepting such ingratitude as his reward. Especially after having searched so diligently for such delicacies as gray mouse *à la Italienne* for his pet!" Amelia spoke with a perfect straight face, belied by the glimmer in her eyes.

Laughing heartily, Justin complimented Amelia on her acceptance of such an unusual pet. "You really permitted a snake in your home? Astonishing. I don't think I know of another woman who would countenance such an unnatural association!"

"They are really quite pleasant, you know. Very clean, require feeding infrequently, and make far less noise than the whippets. Nor do they jump about one's legs or slaver one's face with wet, lapping kisses." She led the way to the door as she spoke. "Quite acceptable, actually, and wonderfully able to speed an unwanted guest on his or her way."

"Speed an unwanted guest?"

"Of course. One just introduces said guest to the snake and nature takes its course. Especially if one hints that the snake might be poisonous!" Amelia laughed with delight at her unmatched plan for ridding herself of the superfluous visitor.

"I hope I never have the misfortune to become one of

those . . . undesirables. Your ingenuity seems to know no bounds." Still laughing, Farnham turned to take his hat from Staunton.

"Mama, Mama, don't leave yet, I must tell you something." A small figure came dashing down the stairs. Unable to stop, the child slid on the polished stone, winding up with his arms wrapped around the earl's long legs.

"Oh—beg pardon, sir. Slippery floor, y'know." A pair of large, apprehensive dark eyes looked up at the earl. "I just have to tell Mama." Perry removed his clasp from the gentleman and ran to his mother. "We caught Cicero and he was so angry he said words that Annie said were very bad. But she laughed!" He raised his arms to his mother to receive the hug he knew she was about to bestow.

"Perry dearest, this is no way to greet the earl. You owe him more courtesy than this!" She smiled down at the eager little face, concealing her trepidation at once again having Farnham see his son.

To her eyes, the resemblance between the two was so apparent that she couldn't believe the earl would be unable to recognize himself in the child.

Courteously, the earl accepted Perry's apology and greeting, then asked him how he was spending his day.

"Oh, Annie and I are going to have a famous time. We're going to the royal menagerie. Dentworth, one of the footmen, told me they have a white tiger there. I've never seen a tiger. Have you?" Before the earl could answer, the child continued, "I don't think I shall be afraid, but if he roars at us, Annie says she'll faint dead away!" Quickly he turned back to his mother. "I must go tell Annie to hurry. G'bye, Mama. G'bye, sir, my lord." Just as quickly, he was away and up the stairs, leaving a pair of breathless, laughing adults in his wake.

Amelia's laughter was as much a result of relief at escaping exposure as response to her son's behavior.

"Your son astounds me with his—what shall I call it?— *joie de vivre*," Justin commented as he handed Amelia up onto the high seat of the phaeton. "He has such aplomb. If it develops, he should stand for Parliament when he grows up. I can just see his enthusiasm and coolness in adversity as he attacks a favored issue. Perhaps he'll carry a few snakes with him!"

The laughter they shared went a long way toward relieving the tension that had existed between them upon greeting each other. They found that they could enjoy each other's company by keeping to innocuous topics of conversation. Gradually they began to question and answer each other about their likes and dislikes, their hopes and fears.

Amelia discovered a man who had a deep and abiding concern for the welfare of his estates and his people. He looked upon his inheritance as a trust to be guarded and developed so that the next heir would have an even greater estate to pass on to the next. It was his belief that this created a continuity of history that gave the country its stability. If one cared not for his own properties, how could he care for his country; it mattered not whether his property was a shepherd's cot or a duke's palace. It was all involved with pride; not the pride of the vain and unworthy, but the pride of achievement in word and deed.

The young woman was amazed to hear her escort speak thus. It seemed incongruous in light of his social behavior. She was not quite able to understand the standards that permitted him to spend such a great proportion of his life gambling, wenching, and living his life in a generally nonproductive way. "Feeling as you do about your inheritance, how is it that you haven't married?" she asked with a sincere desire to understand him.

"What has that to do with anything?" he questioned, suddenly cool in his manner. "There is a perfectly worthy heir, should I not produce one of my own. That *is* the consideration, isn't it?"

"I beg your pardon, my lord. I was carried away by your expression of your philosophy. If your concern is so great, and I commend you for it, it would seem to me it would follow that the survival of your direct line would be of the utmost importance to you. Unless you have a brother to whom you will delegate that responsibility?" Amelia looked at the earl with a raised eyebrow, a smile softening the implied criticism of her question.

"You are too perceptive, Mrs. Carrington . . . Amelia. I

suppose it is just that the institution of marriage hasn't called me to its doors as yet. When I meet a woman who suits my standards, I shall probably wed. But that doesn't have to be for some years yet. The men of my family generally wait until the last minute to find their brides; I shall in all likelihood do the same."

Farnham's statement was like a splash of ice water on Amelia. He had as much as told her that she was not up to his standards, despite their extreme response to each other. For a moment her eyes flashed with strong emotion. Oh, well. She had known he would not offer for her, She was really not in his social bracket—or financial either, for that matter. He would most likely offer for a young heiress of impeccable origins who would have just made her appearance on the marriage mart; one who would be docile and malleable with no prior experience or thoughts of her own. No widow with a child for him. For a long moment she was silent, unable to continue their conversation.

Finally she took a deep breath, almost a sigh, and commenced a commentary on the foibles of some of the more renowned members of the *ton*. "Did you see Lord Willoughby last night? If he persists in dying his hair that unbecoming shade of blond tinged with green, he shall frighten half the pretty young things in London. He minces around holding his quizzing glass to his eye thinking he is as elegant as . . . as . . . *you*, my lord. One wonders how he can make such a cynosure of himself."

"My dear Mrs. Carrington, obviously you were never party to an appearance of Mr. Trilby. He was a gentleman of means whose grandparents were noble parents of an excessively large family. His father was the seventh son so had no claim to a title; however, there was much money. Mr. Trilby made it a practice to wear only jeweled buttons on his coats and waistcoats, and always blue stones to match his blue eyes and his blue clothes."

Amelia started to laugh. "Yes, and probably spoke down to everyone lower than an earl."

"How did you guess? Made it positively unbearable to carry that honor when one was almost always his target." The earl smiled.

The conversation continued in a humorous vein with comments flying back and forth between the two. At times Amelia let her sense of the ridiculous get the better of her and evoked gusts of laughter from the earl. She recounted some of the more florid discussions she had witnessed between otherwise harmless members of the university set when acting as hostess for her husband. As she described the wispy white hairs of one pedant, standing out from his head in a frenzy of anger at another's effrontery in disagreeing with a favored theory about the validity of the secession of the North American colonies from the parent country, the earl was hard put to control his laughter. Her ability to bring to life the people about whom she spoke with a word or phrase or a change in the pronunciation of her words astonished him. Her descriptions were not vindictive; they were more on the order of an exposure of the follies of humanity.

One of the attractions of the young widow, aside from the physical beauty that she displayed, was her freedom from the manners of the ladies of Farnham's acquaintance. She did not try to capture his interest by the affectations of speech, glances, and postures that were considered *de rigueur* by those who wrote the book about flirtation. In fact, she never actually flirted with him. She conversed, laughed at his sallies, disagreed with some of his pronouncements, and in every way conducted herself with a naturalness that was most unusual and appealing. Except for those moments when one or the other was momentarily recalled to the deep attraction that existed between them, they treated each other the way Farnham was accustomed to being treated by his male friends. In fact, he had never had a woman friend other than Eglantine, and she was more the wife of a friend than a friend herself.

For whatever reasons, the two people in the phaeton were more at ease with each other than at any time since they had met at Madame Celeste's salon. The earl attributed it to his confidence in the outcome of the relationship—bedding without wedding, and the enjoyment of Amelia's favors as his mistress. Amelia attributed it to her success in having kept her secret from the earl, not suspecting his determination to offer her *carte blanche*, not allowing herself to contemplate what her answer would be in response to such an action.

The briskly trotting horses had carried them quite a bit farther than the earl had planned. Indeed, his enjoyment of the drive had banished all thought of time and its passing from his mind. Realizing that the short drive he had intended had already occupied more than an hour and that it was close on half after twelve, he suggested to Amelia that they stop for a rest and refreshment at the next public house they should come to. They had long since passed out of the precincts of the park and had been traveling along one of the roads leading out of the metropolis.

"I believe the White Horse Inn is just ahead. We'll be able to get something to drink and eat there," offered the earl. "I had no idea so much time had passed. Your lively humor completely took my mind off the passing of the hours, and now I find we've traveled farther than I had intended. To cap it all off, I'm ravenously hungry. Are you?"

"How nice to know that I can make you laugh with such gusto that you forget to watch the clock." Amelia pretended to preen herself. "My performance has left me with as great a hunger as yours, my lord, and the White Horse is said to set a fine table. This is quite an adventure. And to think I was envying Perry his trip to the menagerie!"

"I had a feeling you would have enjoyed accompanying him today. Shall we pledge to visit that fascinating home of wild beasts on another of our 'drives'?" The earl took his eyes from the road to glance at Amelia's smiling face. "I can't believe I just committed myself to attend a zoological exhibition. You must be a witch and have ensorcel'd me. Do you require a forfeit to release me from this enchantment, witch?" The earl's eyes danced merrily as he enacted his being overcome with fear. "I know, I shall have to find a pure young maiden to release me from the spell." Suddenly his eyes were once more entangled in a lingering look that held Amelia's glowing green eyes captive. Slowly she lifted her hand partway to her face, almost as though to shield herself from the enervating effect of his gaze.

"No ... don't ..." she began. Then, realizing what she had been about to say, she pulled her eyes from his in time to see the horses veering toward the side of the road. "My lord, quickly, the horses!"

"Damnation, what made them do that?" The earl gave vent to his passion by flicking the tip of his whip at the lead horse. "Are you all right? We're beyond lucky that you were watching the road, Amelia. We could easily have landed in the ditch."

"I ... yes ... fortunately the carriage didn't overturn when you swerved the animals. I've noticed that you're a very good driver, my lord, but am very grateful that you are even better than I thought." Amelia fanned herself with her reticule. "I shall really appreciate a glass of wine."

Farnham had pulled into the yard of the small inn and signaled the hostler to take the reins from him. He jumped down from the seat and came around the back of the phaeton to help Amelia descend. Reaching her hand out for his assistance, she carefully lowered her foot to the step and stood up. Somehow her skirts tangled around her other foot, and she tripped into the earl's waiting arms. He held her close for a moment, just long enough for her to feel an attack of weakness of the knees. She made a motion to release herself and was placed gently on her feet, still held, but lightly. She refused to meet his eyes and so did not see the smile that twisted one corner of his mouth. She felt a whisper of a touch as he drew his finger down the side of her face, while murmuring "lovely" in a soft tone. Breathlessly, she removed herself from his vicinity and walked ahead of him into the inn.

Casting instructions at the groom to walk, then water and feed the horses, Farnham followed Amelia into the building.

CHAPTER TWELVE

THE SEVERAL PEOPLE gathered around the table in the coffee room of the inn argued mightily about the ineptitude of the British general in Spain versus the French generals' mistakes in the Russian assault. The voices of the assorted men and one woman were alternately raised and lowered in amicable discussion. All at once a burst of laughter sounded and a look of artless cunning could be seen on the lady's face.

"To be sure, that's the way of it. It always was and always will be a woman's triumph." Amelia finished her statement with an air of exultation and turned to the earl for his approval.

"Gentlemen, we have been outthought, outspoken, and outsmarted by Mrs. Carrington. And now, if you will permit me to thank you all for your discourse, I must return her to her family." With a laugh and a gesture to the innkeeper indicating his desire to settle the tab, Justin rose to help Amelia from her chair.

Words of protest followed the pair as they made their way to the exit, as well as wishes that they might repeat the erudite discussion that had held the disparate group together for the past hour. Farnham had been surprised by the ease with which Amelia had joined the discussion at a table adjacent to theirs in the public room of the inn. She had recognized one of the gentlemen as a former student of her husband's and had renewed his acquaintance. Farnham had felt a stab of annoyance at the smile of pleasure that had lit her face upon seeing the fellow, but when he saw how impartially she treated him, the annoyance faded. The other members of the party had welcomed her presence as soon as they had learned her identity; all had known, or known of, Alfred Carrington and his charming wife, leaders of academic society.

To the earl's amazement, the conversation that followed their arrival at the table ranged over many subjects. Not once was a social event mentioned. Justin came to realize that Amelia's education had been a broad one, learned from the scholars who were experts in their fields. Her mind was bright and her interests diverse. It was intoxicating to find someone with whom one could debate a subject on a level above the rather superficial arguments that one was accustomed to conducting with one's friends. To have that enjoyment enhanced by the tensions that exist between two people who are attracted to each other gave an extra fillip to the event. This was a side that Justin had not previously been privileged to experience in his short acquaintance with Amelia. He could understand her success as the wife of a man in academic circles. In fact, he could see her take her place in any circle where wit and wisdom were requisites. She reminded him of the great courtesans of history. What a salon she could conduct, were she so minded. Perhaps under his guidance, she might become renowned for such things.

The earl pardoned himself a moment from Amelia's side to rouse the hostler and have the horses put to. She stood on the step in front of the inn drawing on her York tan gloves, observing the activities that were necessary to harness two lively horses. The bright sun drew reddish glints from the tawny hair that escaped the confines of her charming hat and sparks from her green eyes. The breeze blew gently, pressing the cloth of her garments to her body, outlining her rounded hips and long, slender legs. As the earl strolled over to her to help her to the ready phaeton, he sensed a feeling of *déjà vu,* almost as though he had once before faced this woman in the same way, under the same circumstances. His pulses quickened at her loveliness. Who did she remind him of? The question puzzled him for a moment and then was forgotten in the heady presence of her fragrance.

Once again Amelia was benumbed by the electricity of the earl's glance as her eyes caught his. With great effort she broke the spell and made a comment on the speed with which the groom had worked. Farnham placed his hand under her arm to conduct her across the cobbled yard, burning her skin with his touch. At the carriage he put his hands on her waist to aid her in her ascent, but neither was able to move. The slight tremor of her body conveyed its message to him; he was hard put to keep from enfolding her in his arms then and there. Amelia felt the strength go from her legs and leaned back against the earl's chest, too weak to move. If he had turned her and led her back into the inn and into a bedchamber, she would have been helpless to prevent him. She wanted nothing more than to resume the game of love they had played with such passion and perfection. She was almost ready to take the chance that he would have forgotten the birthmark or would forgive her her deception. Almost.

Overcoming his desire to embrace Amelia, Farnham threw her up onto the seat of the vehicle and quickly jumped up beside her. He flipped a coin to the groom as he turned the horses and headed them out of the inn's courtyard. Amelia remained motionless on the seat. She was alternately joyous and miserable, alternately fighting off the backlash of her feelings and relishing the sensations that stimulated her.

Justin had time to plan his next move on the long drive

back to Princess Gardens. He was determined to make
Amelia his mistress and to that end decided to reopen the
little house that had not been used since that last visit so
many years ago—when he found a note ending his affair
with the one woman he had ever met who had the power
to tie him to her with bonds that went beyond mere infatuation.

The result of that unresolved affair had been a lingering
anger; he had felt abandoned and ridiculed by a woman to
whom he had been ready to offer his name. So enamored
had he been of his "Lady Mystère" that he had been ready
to speak the marriage vows with her, not even knowing her
real name and lineage. That, for the proud earl, was the
greatest gift he could have given to a woman; she had never
known because she had never again met him.

He had been left with a distaste for what he thought of
as his weakness. That he had forgotten himself so far as to
even contemplate marriage with an unknown was folly
enough, but that he had allowed himself to fall in love was
the epitome of fatuity. Never again would he permit himself
to be blinded by such weakness; never again would he offer
marriage where his senses were overly engaged. No, marriage must be a hard-headed business coalition between two
names. The woman involved would not matter other than
as the mother of his children; both would understand the
freedom they could command in such a relationship once
the heir had been produced.

By the time the phaeton drew up in front of 52 Princess
Gardens, Amelia had decided to take a gamble that would
settle the situation between herself and Justin one way or
the other. She could no longer face the present uncertainty.
Better to confess her past imposture and know whether or
not her beloved would understand. If he turned from her,
then so be it; but if he believed her story and accepted her
love, then heaven would be hers.

As he helped her down from the carriage, she banished
the weakness his touch brought her. "Justin . . . my lord . . ."
she began, with difficulty.

"Justin sounds well from your lips" was his response.

"Justin, we must talk. . . ." She looked up at him, entreaty in her eyes. "Would you come in with me? We must have a moment. Please . . ."

"Certainly, Amelia." He tucked her hand in the crook of his elbow. "There is something I have to speak to you about also. Perhaps it's the same thing."

Once more the earl handed his hat and gloves to Staunton with a comment about the chilly October day. After divesting herself of her pelisse, Amelia instructed her major-domo to see that she and the earl were not interrupted for the next twenty minutes. After that he could have tea served in the drawing room.

She quickly slipped past the tall, urbane man, leading him into the library. She held the door open until he had entered and then closed it against interruption. With a thoughtful air, she turned to speak to Farnham, only to find him standing immediately behind her. She caught her breath at their closeness, overcome by a wave of desire. She swayed toward the man and was caught in his arms, enveloped in the embrace that was her heart's home. Her hands reached up to entwine themselves behind his head, pulling him toward her. In the moment that seemed to take forever but lasted only an instant, they reached, the one for the other, mingling their breath in a deep, consuming kiss. Time stopped and started again before Justin lifted his mouth from Amelia's. She attempted to push away from him but his grip tightened, pulling her into an even closer embrace. She felt as though he was drinking the breath from her body, replacing it with an effervescent substance that bubbled in her veins and intoxicated her senses. She pressed against him, needing the strength of his muscular body to support her failing balance. First roughly, then gently he fondled her, letting his hands move over her breasts and hips, devouring her with passion.

Breathless, hair tousled, cheeks flushed, Amelia began to pull away. "Justin, Justin . . . you must stop. Please, I must talk to you." She took his hands and held them away from her body. "You must stop. Anyone could come in here. . . ."

Equally flushed, the earl finally awoke to the extremes to which he had almost been carried. He turned his back to her and then moved away from her so that the distance of the room was between them.

"I couldn't help myself . . . I must have you. I need you more than I've ever needed anyone before." Justin was astonished at his words. Always before carrying on a flirtation with a coolness and calculatedness that inevitably brought him his prize, he was literally begging this woman—this witch—to accommodate his ardor. He watched her lift her arms to rewind the heavy coil of hair that had become loosened in the vigor of his embrace. He had never seen anything so seductive as the straining of the fabric of her dress across her breasts and the graceful movements of her arms as she worked to pin her hair in place.

"Justin, I have something very important to tell you." Amelia paused, rehearsing in her mind the succession of words she must put together to tell her lover the truth about their past romance. "Many years ago, I—"

Before she could continue, she heard a knock at the door and Staunton's voice saying her name. The door opened and the middle-aged retainer announced the arrival of Lord and Lady Dunmore and Sir Richard Dyckman. His announcement was followed by the entrance of the principals named: Lady Dunmore, bustling and talkative, a tiny little bird of a woman, made a sharp contrast to her huge, six-foot husband. They had been close friends of Alfred Carrington's, and Lady Dunmore had been very kind to the newlywed Amelia. She spoke in pronouncements that had the effect of being royal observations and commands, an affectation she had that was designed to give importance to her diminutive frame. She had once told Amelia that she had had to develop a voice the size of her husband's body in order to hold her own against him.

"My dear gel, I knew you wouldn't mind our arriving at this house. Sir Richard met us just as we were about to return home and mentioned that he intended visiting you so we decided to join him. Such a good idea, don't you know. And Farnham, so nice to see you also. Didn't expect to find you here, thought you only drove in the mornings." As Justin and Amelia exchanged a long glance, Lady Dunmore's big voice continued on about the fortuitousness of having met Sir Richard. Justin's eyebrow lifted slightly as though to say "Well, what can one do?" Amelia smiled slightly and was thankful that she and Farnham had not been caught in that very revealing interlude. She was still suffering from the aftereffect, but listening to Lady Dunmore was like taking a cold bath—passion was quickly reduced to a giggle.

Silently, Sir Richard observed the two people who had been in the room alone a few minutes before. The precipitous entrance of Lady Dunmore, followed by her husband and himself, had found Farnham and Amelia at opposite ends of the room, but there had been a tension between them that deeply disturbed him. If he were to put his feelings into words, he would say that he perceived the earl was ready to make an offer to Amelia. He was more than ready to give odds that the offer was not for marriage; either kind of proposition left him less than pleased. He still felt that Amelia would make an admirable ambassador's wife, but if she wouldn't have him, he would almost rather see her marry anyone than become Farnham's plaything.

"Oh, dear Lady Dunmore, Lord Dunmore, and Richard, I *am* glad to see you. I had intended to leave my card tomorrow, my lady; Perry has been begging me to take him with me so he can see your grandson again." Amelia actually felt relief at the arrival of the older couple. She had almost succumbed to Justin's embraces. Another few minutes and who knew what the Dunmores would have found when they arrived so unexpectedly. Despite the burden of her lacerated senses, Amelia had to smile. What better cure for such a scene than the very people who had arrived.

"Amelia, my dear, I couldn't wait to see you. Buffy and I"—Lady Dunmore turned to indicate her husband—"feel a responsibility to Alfred to see you're getting along. How is dear Perry? Such an active child. I have told my daughter that town life is very deleterious to children. She should keep them in the country at all times. Don't you agree?"

Without waiting for an answer, Lady Dunmore continued: "Dear girl, I do believe you're looking a bit pale. Not enough walking. You must take long walks. Especially in the country . . . which brings me to my news; we are having a house-party and hunt. We've planned it to begin two weeks from tomorrow and to last two weeks and think you and Perry would enjoy coming with us. My daughter and her husband will be there with their children which provide a couple of youngsters for Perry to get into mischief with." Lady Dunmore was a doting grandmother and took every opportunity to have her grandchildren with her.

"As for yourself, the weather should be perfect for the hunt, and if I remember correctly, you're a bruising rider. I expect you haven't had a good gallop since you arrived." She named some others who had accepted invitations to the party and urged Amelia to join the group. "Farnham is coming." She looked to the earl for corroboration. "Aren't you, my lord? And Sir Richard and Eglantine and her husband. A few older people; not for the hunt, but most congenial. Do say you'll join us, my dear." The tiny woman smiled kindly at Amelia.

At first Amelia hesitated, not knowing how her affair with Justin would proceed, then she decided that it might do him good to see her with other possible suitors. After all, although she could love no other, he was not the only fish in the sea; other men found her attractive. Perhaps he would feel the tiniest bit of jealousy. Her lips curved in a secret smile at the thought of arousing a fierce emotion in Justin's breast.

He would also have more time with Perry. That might help. If not, why, then she might just decide to end the whole thing. Even though he stirred her as he did, one couldn't live on excitement alone. There were such things as tenderness and consideration and . . . She awoke to her duties as hostess when Lady Dunmore commented on her abstraction.

"I've been thinking of your kind invitation. Unless I remember incorrectly, I've no other engagements then, and Perry and I would love to join your party. Naturally I shall bring my own horse and Perry's pony."

Amelia continued conversing with Lady Dunmore about the plans for her houseparty. At the same time she watched Farnham chatting with Lord Dunmore and Sir Richard. She exclaimed over the rout the Dunmore's had planned and commiserated with her hostess-to-be on the illness of her French chef, which had necessitated hiring a new person for the party.

Amelia's concentration was centered on the earl's relaxed figure, lounging in an oversized wingchair with no hint on his face of their brief, passionate encounter. He was discussing the relative merits of the Quorn versus the Melton hunts, Lord Dunmore holding out for the Quorn since it was run over a more hazardous course, thus offering more excitement. Abruptly the earl pulled a watch from his pocket and rose from the chair.

"I am recalled to another engagement and must beg leave to say good-bye. Lord and Lady Dunmore, always a pleasure to see you." He bent courteously to the couple as he murmured words of farewell. "Sir Richard, we should have dinner together one evening, renew old friendships and such. Mrs. Carrington, will you keep me company to the door?" He extended his arm to Amelia, who took it with an apologetic glance at her other guests.

"How could you embarrass me like that?" she whispered when they reached the foyer. "Really, you take too much for granted."

"Do I?" The earl looked at her with a slight smile. "I had to get you away to make arrangements with you for tomorrow. We have some unfinished business to . . . discuss? Shall you ride with me? Early."

Amelia's heart began to beat erratically. Why did he put it in such a way? "I was not aware we had unfinished business," she said, attempting a degree of hauteur.

"You know very well that we have much to talk of . . . and . . . decisions to make. I shall be here at nine. Be ready." He would not brook no for an answer.

Suddenly Amelia's eyes sparkled with anger. She drew her slim figure to its full height. "You *do* take too much for granted, sir. I am not sure I'm free tomorrow morning." She began to move away from him, but he reached for her arm, bringing her to a stop. His hand slid down to hers. His sensuous mouth moved in a disarming smile. "How can you be so cruel, Goddess? Not ten minutes ago your lips gave me a promise. Albeit without words, 'twas a promise."

By now overcome with the need to be with him, and having already made the decision to tell him that she was his Lady of the Masque, Amelia consented to join him in the morning. She could no longer bear the feeling of being on the edge of a sword, waiting for him to recognize her. At her agreement, Farnham lifted her hand to his lips, touching the palm with his tongue in an intimate gesture. She gasped at the stab of lightning that ran up her arm and pulled her hand away, furious that this man affected her so. Before she could admonish him, he ran lightly out the door and jumped onto the seat of his waiting phaeton.

Staunton closed the door, looking at Amelia questioningly. His little Melly was having problems, and he didn't like it one bit. She refused to answer his gaze, merely shrugged her shoulders, then returned to the drawing room and her guests.

Lord and Lady Dunmore were ready to take their leave soon after. There was more chatter about the coming houseparty, with arrangements for Annie, Staunton, and Kenton to make. Lady Dunmore assured Amelia that she would send her a list of the entertainments planned so that she would be able to bring the appropriate wardrobe, but she emphasized the informality of the occasion. Only one rout, two card parties, and a rather large dinner and dance were being planned at the moment. Of course, there would probably be some evening visits to various gentry in the surrounding area, but no elaborate toilette was needed. One never did need an elaborate couture in the country. But riding habits, that was more the thing. She should bring several habits. Unless there was rain, there would be riding every day.

Trailing instructions and followed by a silent husband, Lady Dunmore finally left the room. Exhausted by the detailed charges issued by the energetic lady, Amelia collapsed, laughing, into a chair.

"She absolutely prostrates me. So much vitality for such a small person. It's no wonder Lord Dunmore says so little. No one can get a word in edgewise when she's around! And yet she's so kind, so thoughtful, in between speeches." Amelia fanned herself with her hand. "I hope I have the stamina to enjoy her company for a week or more."

"At least she has made you laugh, Amelia," said Sir Richard. "It seemed to me you weren't feeling well when we arrived. Not all the thing." Sir Richard took a seat on the sofa next to Amelia's chair. "I hope nothing Lord Croyville said or did caused you unease. He has an unusual effect on ladies." The diplomat in him forced caution in his speech, but the memory of her dazed green eyes when she had greeted him earlier gave rise to a need to declare himself to her.

"And just what do you mean to imply, Sir Richard? Think you that I am some sapskull to be taken in by the manners of a rake? For surely that is what you are hinting." Amelia softened her acerbic words with a smile. "I am not a debutante to be taken in by Lord Croyville's fascinating ways, nor by any man's, dear sir. Should I wish to reply to a man's attentions with certain kindnesses, he would know *before he asked* that those kindnesses were forthcoming. And should I dream to be bespoused, I would share my dream in such a way that the man of my choice would have no hesitation in declaring himself." She kept her eyes down demurely, glancing at him sideways from under half-closed lids. "So, dear sir, you have naught to fear about my impressions of Justin Farnham. I know exactly what kind of effect he has on impressionable ladies, and I am not one of them."

"Certainly not, I never for a moment thought you were, dear Amelia." Sir Richanrd changed his mind about asking for the lady's hand in marriage, at least for this day. She was obviously not ready to give him the answer he was hoping for. In fact, as he examined the words she had just spoken, he came to the conclusion that she might never be ready to give it. And yet she didn't turn him away altogether; best continue on as they were. He would act the friend so that she would know she had him to count on should she have need of his services at any time. It was too bad that the explosive relationship he sensed between the earl and the widow would have time to reach maturity. Certainly it could only lead to heartbreak for Amelia; she seemed inclined to commit herself more fully to a relationship than Farnham.

"I find I must leave, dear lady." Sir Richard stood with his hand on Amelia's shoulder, looking down into her eyes. "It would be fruitless for me to say anything else on the matter, wouldn't it? You know how I feel."

Amelia put her hand over his. "Dear Sir Richard. For now let us be friends. Friendship is often a more satisfying relationship than the chaotic one of . . . that which you wish for. Come, let me walk with you to the door." She rose and took his arm, saying with affection, "I think the Dunmore houseparty should be a triumph of entertainment, don't you? Shall you join the hunt? I've heard that you are supposed to go to Russia for the meeting with the czar. Surely that will be a terribly long journey." With the ease of a diplomat herself, Amelia changed the subject before sending her friend on his way. She listened to his short replies, nodding and talking as she stepped along beside him. "Don't be unhappy, Richard," she finally said. "The habit of single-ness is too deeply engrained in you for you to be happy with a wife. And just think, now you can continue to have your liaisons without fearing discovery by your angry spouse!" She laughed aloud at the rueful smile she caught on his face.

"You are a rogue, Amelia. And I love you for it."

"I hope I may always be a rogue, Richard, and deserve your love. Good-bye for now. I shall see you at Covent Garden for the *School for Scandal* performance, shall I not?"

"You may count on it" were the gentleman's parting words as he walked out the door.

CHAPTER THIRTEEN

THE NEXT DAY Amelia rose somewhat hollow-eyed from lack of sleep. She had spent much of the night creating scenes between herself and Justin. Some were loving, passionate, kind; others were cold, cruel, an affliction to her spirit. She knew she would accept whatever the earl offered her. Her infatuation was complete; she no longer had the strength of will to deny him. In the light of his appetite for her kisses on the previous day and her equal ardor in returning them, she had little hope that he would offer her his name.

Slowly and carefully she dressed herself. Her black velvet riding habit with the jacket *à la hussar* fit her body to perfection. Trim black boots shod her feet, and a dashing black top hat sat on her head, tilted over her right eye. There was no touch of color in her costume; the only color was the green of her eyes, enormous in her pale face. She touched her neck with perfume, and the inner surface of her wrists, then defiantly she opened her jacket and dabbed some scent on the skin between her breasts. She had left off her stays and wore only a chemise and petticoat beneath her habit, blushing as she labeled herself wanton.

Before she descended to the foyer, she tried to swallow some coffee, but she couldn't get any down. She gave up the effort and ran quickly out of her room and down the stairs, preferring to be mounted on her horse, waiting outside for her escort. Before she was able to exit the house, Annie called her name.

"Miss Melly, I must speak to you. I know what you're doing and I must speak with you first. Please come to my room where we can be private, my honey girl. Please?" Annie's eyes were shiny with tears.

It was beyond Amelia's ability to refuse the woman who had cared for her so diligently for most of her life. "All right, Annie, but don't read me a lecture. I've made up my mind." Without discussion, the younger woman knew what was disturbing Annie.

Quietly, Annie led the way to the little room that was her sanctum, then stood looking at Amelia, examining her features as though trying to read her mind.

"When you were a little girl," she began, "you were the most easygoing child, as long as what we wanted for you to do was what *you wanted* to do. I don't think anyone ever realized that until the time you were told not to ride your father's new horse. You agreed, we thought, although you never said so in words. You spoke of hearing what we were saying or something such that didn't actually commit you to doing as we had told you. You truly gulled us, young as you were, and you rode the horse and broke your arm when you were thrown. Are you doing the same thing to yourself now, Miss Melly? Are you gulling yourself into breaking your heart? You have more than yourself to think about. What about Perry? What about your good name? It's all you have to offer a man, and if you go to *him*, you won't have that for very long.

"And what will you do when he finds out about Perry? Do you think he'll be pleased? He's a proud man, not priggish but quick to take offense, I think, if he considers himself to have been taken for a fool. Not one to forgive easily. Have you given thought to that, my dearie?"

Had Amelia not thought the same things that Annie was so forcefully reminding her of, she would have screamed her defiance at the conventions of society. As it was, she acknowledged Annie's concern, then said: "I love him. Not just for the moment shared in bed but for everything that he is—even for his pride. I would rather have him know and hate me than to fear his learning afterward. That he could never forgive. But I hope only that when he hears me out and knows that I did what I did for both my loves, he will forgive me. Then I will do whatever he wants. If I should be so fortunate as to have him offer me his name, you know I would take him. But if he asks me only to be his mistress, I will accept that also, for I must have him on any terms. I am shameless where he is concerned. Does that make me a wicked woman, Annie?"

"No, my dearest, you could never be wicked." Annie's tone of voice changed then. "You're just stupid and that's worse. You'll ruin yourself. I beg you not to do this thing. Go away from him for a while before you decide." Tears began to streak down her cheeks. "My little Melly, I'm afeart that you're in for a terrible heartbreak, and there's no way you can avoid it if you go to him and tell him now."

"I know, Annie, but I can't help myself. I think I always knew this would happen if ever I met him again. As long as Alfred was alive and we lived where there was no possibility of that happening, I was safe. Once we returned to London and I saw him again, the game was lost. Don't worry. If it works out, I shall be the happiest woman alive; and if it doesn't, well, at least I will be able to stop living this kind of 'not knowing' life." Gently the woman put her arms around her nurse and kissed her cheek, brushing the hair back from her forehead. "I must go now. He'll be waiting for me."

Justin was standing at the foot of the steps as she walked

out the door, watching her gracefully pick up the long train of the velvet skirt. He remarked on her paleness and the green of her eyes, startling against her pallid skin.

He reached out his hand to help her, saying, "Good morning. I expected to have to wait for you."

Her eyes clung to his. "I was up early. The weather is so fine I thought I would wait for you outdoors." Her eyelids fluttered down, unable to sustain the warmth of his gaze.

"It's rather nice weather for this time of year." He placed his hands on her waist to lift her into the saddle, feeling the heat of her body through the fabric of her habit; his blood was fired by the sensation.

"How are you feeling today?" The words left her throat with difficulty. She pressed her knee against her mount and led the way into the street.

All the time they were making innocuous remarks, there was the knowledge of the unspoken sentiments. Their awareness of each other was so intense that the outer world became a peripheral annoyance. They had ridden almost to St. James Park before the earl started to speak. He had moved his horse up so that he was riding at Amelia's side.

"Amelia, listen to me. You must know how I feel. I am distracted by your beauty; you are constantly in my thoughts, and when we're together I want you in my arms. Each time I've kissed you it's been hell to have to stop. You must come with me today." He studied her face for a moment, waiting for her to speak. When she said nothing, he continued with his plea. "Ordinarily I wouldn't do this with such crudity; I'm used to playing at the game of love with more finesse. I would talk about the tender passion I have formed for you; I would tell you that you are my lady love, my angel, my goddess. And then I would wait for you to express your partiality for me when I have presented you with a suitable gift. But I can't do that with you. This is no game I am playing. I wish to have you, and I know you feel the same way about me. It's not as though you are newly come on the scene of love. You must feel the passion I feel. Your kisses tell me you do." Still the woman to whom he was declaring himself did not speak. "We have the opportunity to be alone now for a few ... an hour or two. No one will expect you back before two hours. Let us escape the boredom of the day. Escape with me to a special little haven where we can give each other more joy than you've ever dreamed of."

Amelia hesitated; she had not expected him to be so forthright about his desires. She realized now that he was offering her, or would offer her, no more than *carte blanche*, the honor of becoming his mistress. If he still wanted that after she told him about the past, she would agree. But wait; perhaps he wouldn't remember the birthmark. Perhaps it would be better to just accept his offer for today and see what happened. It might be the better move; once he was more attached to her he might not mind at all about their previous liaison. She decided to take the gamble.

"Stop a moment. I must look at you when I say this, Justin." She reined in her horse and waited for him to face her. "I will go with you. I would go with you to the ends of the earth if you asked me. I have no pride where you are concerned because I love you with all my heart. I expect no more from you than you can give me, but never speak of payment, never give me gifts. When it's over, it will be over—either today or tomorrow or next year. Let us enjoy this ... passion ... for what it is until then." She spoke quietly, firmly, and with an honesty that astounded the earl.

"If these are your conditions, my dear, I accept them." He smiled at last, the triumphant male unable to conceal his sense of victory. And Amelia smiled also—a small, sad smile.

The two rode side by side through the park into one of the small streets that led to their destination. It was the same house to which he had brought his lady of mystery years ago, only now the shrubs were quite overgrown and there was a somewhat unkept look about the neat brick building. Someone had cleaned the walkway and the path to the stable, making it easy for them to ride their horses around before dismounting. There were no stablehands present so Justin dismounted, then went to help Amelia off her horse. He held his arms up to reach for her. She placed her hands on his shoulders and leaned forward, ready to slide from her saddle. He grasped her around the waist, firmly easing her from her perch until he held her against his body. They stood that way for a moment, lost in the thunder of their pulses. Before he let her go, he bent his lips to hers, losing himself in her kiss. They were enclosed by the overgrown shrubbery, the occasional sounds from the street deadened by the dense evergreens, creating a world apart in which they stood enraptured.

With a great effort she disengaged from him, murmuring that they should go inside, saying something about having to speak to him about something very important. Once again she had changed her mind about telling him. It went against the grain to continue a lie that had begun without thought of hurting anyone except perhaps herself. He responded to her plea by kissing her again, this time turning her so that they could walk as they embraced. He raised his head finally, saying softly that he had only to light the fire once they were inside and she would feel more comfortable. There would be plenty of time for talk later.

As Farnham opened the door with a great brass key, Amelia pulled away from his side, almost running into the chilly hall. The windows were overgrown with ivy, making the foyer dark when the door was closed. The earl muttered an oath when he was unable to find the lucifers to light the candles in the wall sconces, then he remembered that there was a box of them next to the fireplace in the small parlor.

Amelia stood still in the entryway. The faint smell of the house was a blend of perfume and cigar smoke and a hint of dampness. It was an odor more of disuse, unopened windows and lack of sunlight, but it took her back to the last time she had stood there—almost seven years ago. She remembered the feverish excitement of that visit; she had known it was to be her last time with Justin and had been determined to give him and herself a memory that they would never forget. She couldn't answer for him, but she had never forgotten the heights of ecstasy that she had reached that night, made the more intense for knowing she would never experience such emotion again.

Flickering light cast by the flames from the fire that had finally taken in the fireplace began to reflect from the walls. Justin came back to the hall to take her hand and lead her into the parlor. He sat her in a chair beside the fire where she would feel the heat of the flames.

"Stay here while I light the fires in the other room. The caretaker hasn't been here today so the house has a chill in it. I shall be right back." He ran his fingers over her mouth before he walked slowly away from her.

Amelia looked around at the once-familiar room. The furniture was still the same, a little faded with the air of a past elegance and disuse. The chamber had been dusted but was not cared for. She remembered how clean and sparkling it had once been, and wondered if Justin still used it as often as he had then. This little house was his trysting place and probably had been known to many women. Had any of them loved him as much as she had? Certainly none had come into the house with as little knowledge of love or left with as much.

"Are you feeling any warmer?" the earl asked as he reentered the room. "Come with me. You shall definitely feel warmer presently. There are two fireplaces in the bed-chamber." He laughed softly at the deep blush that covered Amelia's cheeks and forehead. "What's this? Don't let yourself feel embarrassment. You love me, remember?"

"I must speak to you, Justin. It's important. I—" Amelia tried to speak but was stopped by the earl as he swept her up into his arms and once again placed his lips on hers.

Her arms crept around his neck and helplessly she let herself become lost in the ardent pressure of his mouth on hers. He carried her into the bedroom, sitting down with her on an ottoman near the fire. He held her in place with his lips, forcing her mouth open to accept the tip of his tongue slowly caressing the softness of hers. She felt a flame flare up in the pit of her belly, sending its heat swiftly through her body. His fingers were unfastening the buttons of her jacket, then slipping the garment from her shoulders. He took his hot mouth from hers, placing it on the pliant white skin just beneath her collar bone and letting it move in soft nips down to the edge of her chemise.

She was helpless in his arms, wanting the tremors never to end. Skillfully he unfastened her skirt and, raising her slightly from his lap, slipped both skirt and petticoat off. Without stopping the kisses that were exciting her so, he began to undo his cravat, murmuring to her to help him unfasten his shirt. Their bodies pressed against each other, burrowing together as their hands struggled to release him from his garments. Their need for each other was so great that it was impossible for one to let go of the other. The earl stood, still holding Amelia close, and moved to the bed, murmuring words of endearment, praising the beauties of her body. The only light in the room came from the two fires at either end of the chamber, bathing the occupants in a soft glow, creating shadows of mystery on their bodies.

He placed her on the bed and lay down beside her, covering her mouth with his, letting his hands play on those shadowed mysteries. Their passion reached a frenzy of sensation, until they both cried out in release and clung together until the descent from the heights allowed them to speak once again.

Their bodies still entwined, they shared a kiss of pleasure, thanking each other for the rapture they had shared. Softly they fondled each other, stroking and kissing in the aftermath of passion. They asked and answered with words, with eyes, with hands whether this pleased more or that gave more pleasure. Justin looked at Amelia, her lips swollen with kisses, cheeks flushed with love. Carefully he moved himself from above her to gaze at her body, wanting to devour with his eyes that which he had just enjoyed with his body. He relished the softness of her flesh, the fullness of her breasts. Tenderly he smoothed his hands over them, watching her luxuriate in the sensuousness of his touch. He turned his eyes down as she moved over onto her side, exposing the underpart of her breast. Suddenly his hand stopped its motion as a feeling of coldness came over him.

"What's this mark?" His voice was suddenly changed. "Where came you this? Is it a birthmark or an injury? Tell me!"

Amelia felt as though she couldn't breathe. How to tell him without alienating him? She was helpless. It was unavoidable. She must tell him now. If only she hadn't let him persuade her, but what could she have said in the face of his, and her, consuming need.

"I . . . please Justin, my dearest, please let me explain. . . ." She couldn't bring herself to speak until she could gauge his temper.

"You . . . you were my lady Mystère, but why did you disappear without a word? Why didn't you ever tell me who you were? You spoke with an accent. I thought you were French." His face was puzzled, still smiling, but not sparkling with the same kind of excitement she had seen just a moment before. "Oh, God! I'm overwhelmed that I've found you. Amelia, my sweetheart. You'll never know how I longed for you. But why did you disappear?" Even though he moved closer, thrusting his head toward hers, she could feel his withdrawal. His black brows drew together as he awaited an answer. Then before she could formulate one adequate to the urgency of his tone, his questions began again, gaining intensity as he voiced his thoughts.

"Where did you go? Why did you carry on such a masquerade? What kind of a fool did you take me for? I had fallen in love with you, was ready to make you my wife, and you disappeared without a word of explanation."

Somewhere in her head she could hear her voice screaming, "Oh, God, don't let this happen. I love him! I love him!"

His words scorched her with the heat of his anger. "What kind of woman are you to have let me suffer like that? And then when I met you again, could you not have told me? Did you think you would control me as the virtuous Mrs. Carrington? Perhaps you meant to ensnare me in marriage? 'Justin, I love you . . . no gifts, no money . . .'" His voice was like a whip, lacerating her with its sting as he threw her words back at her.

"Let me explain, Justin, please. I tried to tell you but the time never seemed right. Oh, please listen to me." The joy that had shone from her eyes had changed to anguish in the face of his rising anger. She sat up in the bed, the warm color from the fire reflecting from her satiny skin. He was on the bed next to her, half kneeling, half rising. "I meant it when I said I loved you. There were reasons why I had to disappear. I was married."

"Yes, I realize now that you were married. It must have been a lark carrying on with another man while your husband was away. Perhaps he couldn't satisfy your lascivious nature, and you had to look elsewhere for your pleasure."

"Oh, no, don't say such things!" Her eyes were large with horror at the change in her lover.

"Since that is what you wanted, my lady, then let me give you more pleasure. I wouldn't wish to deprive you. You must be hungry, you found it so easy to accept my invitation." As he castigated Amelia, her beauty stimulated his senses once again, and he allowed his eyes to linger over her charms. Her firm breasts, round hips, and smooth thighs had given him more pleasure than he could remember having enjoyed before; now they aroused him but his desire was to hurt her, to give her pain, to humiliate her. He told himself that her response to his lovemaking had been a performance, a betrayal of the ecstasy they had seemed to share. As he worked himself up, he submerged the civilized man and allowed the primitive beast to take over. He threw himself at the now-apprehensive woman, covering her mouth with a brutal kiss.

She pushed him away, crying, "Justin, don't . . . don't do this to me! Please . . ."

The lovely endearments that he had murmured to her in their passion now became taunts about her character and moral persuasions. "Whore, lovely whore, you shall know how to feed your hunger." Cruelly he handled her body where less than fifteen minutes before he had adored her. The polished, skillful lover became a product of the jungle.

At the touch of his hands on her, Amelia felt the difference and fought to move away from him. He twisted a hand in her hair, holding her head still to receive his bruising kisses. Her body was trapped by his leg, and the more she twisted and turned to escape him, the more savage he became.

Finally, recognizing that her resistance only served to arouse his anger more, she lay still and let him have his will with her. The tears that trickled down the sides of her face were the tears of a heart that was breaking. At the same time, they were tears of anger at herself for being so gullible as to believe that this man whom she had literally worshipped would have the generosity to believe her and forgive her. Her arms were outstretched on the bed, fists clenched, but as the assault on her body continued, she was unable to prevent herself from moving to his rhythm. Her body was aroused against her will. As she was crying out to him to stop, her arms and hands urged him on. Once more she cried out and then broke into a storm of weeping. The earl rolled off her quivering form, still keeping her captive with an arm across her waist. She lay still for a moment, feeling his arm relax its hold, then with a speed that pushed her exhausted body to the limit of its endurance, she pushed him away and jumped off the bed.

Now her rage broke through. "You fool! What you have lost you will never know. You, who call yourself a gentleman. What do you know of gentleness? I came to you because I have loved you for seven years. What I did before I did to honor a husband who wanted more than anything in the world to have a child. And I thought to use you to that end." Her voice was harsh as she spat the words at him. "But the Lady of Mystery fooled herself and fell in love with the man she had chosen so carefully to father her child. Yes, my lord Croyville, I fell in love with you, became infatuated, couldn't wait for your touch, the fire you produced in me, and the ecstasy you shared with me. But my lord, what does a wife do in this instance when she honors her husband and has no wish to make him suffer? She cuts out the sickness, for that is how I taught myself to consider that consuming desire I felt for you—for your mind, your heart and your body."

As she spoke, Amelia was pulling on her clothes. "You had no such thoughts about me, my lord. I was a passing fancy, a caprice to while away a few hours. So I gave you up—without warning, without ease. But I took with me your seed. Oh, yes, my lord, I was successful in my quest.

I had my child, a beautiful little son to give my husband.

"I was going to offer my son to you—for he's your son too. But never, *never* will I do that now. I wouldn't allow him to spit on you, Justin Farnham. He is no longer your son. He is mine and the son of the man who cared for him.

"You are as the dirt beneath my feet from this moment on, and I hope you live to regret the love you've torn from my heart. Let your pride give you the caresses, the tenderness, the affection that you might have found with me, that I would have given you as your mistress or your wife, whichever you had offered." Amelia began to laugh. "To imagine I was going to give up everything to give you my love and my son! What a fool, what a hopeless fool!" She whirled and ran from the room, leaving the earl frozen by her revelations.

Twisting up her hair and jamming it under her hat, Amelia headed for the stable, tripping and stumbling as she went. The horses had never been unsaddled. She and her paramour had been too impetuous in their lust to have taken the time for such labor. Her thoughts were filled with disgust at herself. Her battered sensibilities had overcome her innate sense. The shock of the earl's cruel brutality had given her the energy to remove herself from his presence, but now that she was mounted and galloping down the road toward home, she had difficulty staying on her horse. She wanted to run from herself, from him, from the world. Almost she wanted to kill herself at the loss of her dream, but the thought of Perry saved her from that. She avoided the more traveled streets and finally arrived at Princess Gardens. Throwing the reins of her horse to the porter sweeping the steps, she ran into the house, disheveled and weeping, crying for Annie.

At the sight of the worried face, loving and constant, Amelia flung her arms about the buxom woman, crying, "I lost, Annie, I lost," and then fainted away in an excess of emotion.

"Oh, my poor little girl. I tried to tell you, but you wouldna listen." The devoted servant gathered the unconscious woman in her arms, calling for Staunton to come and carry her to her bedroom.

CHAPTER FOURTEEN

"SHE WAS CRYING again last night, and she doesn't want to have Perry about. I'm that worried, John, I'm fair losing my mind." Annie was sharing her worries with her staunch friend. "She's hard, cold. If I had it in my power to horsewhip that man for whatever he did or said to my little Melly, I would be at him in a trice. What are we going to do? It's been three days since she came back in such a state, and it's worse now than it was."

Staunton shook his head. "I've been thinking on it. Perhaps we should call on Lady Winterset, she that was such a friend to Melly when they was at school together. You could go to see her and ask her to pay a visit on our girl."

"There are bruises on her body, Staunton. You can see his fingermarks. I can remember when she told me about him seven years ago. She was half in love with him before she ever met him and could only tell me that he had a reputation for being gentle with the ladies. If it was that way then, 'tis that way no longer. He treated her cruel, he did." Annie moved the cups and plates about on the little table as she spoke. "Ah, it breaks my heart to see her so." A sob escaped her throat.

"Now, now, Annie. Stop dithering about with the dishes. You'll have a pile of broken crockery on the floor before you're through, and then you'll start to cry about that. Here, take hold of yourself and pour me another cup of tea."

The two were having their noonday meal together in the empty kitchen. The kitchen cat lay sunning itself on the windowsill, its purring timed by the ticking of the kitchen clock hanging on the wall next to the oven. The room had the quiet comfort that some kitchens seem to offer.

"I'm sorry, John. Would you like some more to eat? A piece of pie?" Annie rose to fetch the kettle from the hearth. "Here, I'll just make up a fresh pot o' tea for you." As she moved about the room, she sighed deeply and shook her head in despair. "Maybe you're right, John. Maybe I should speak to Lady Winterset. She seems such a practical woman, young as she is. Maybe she'll be able to get Melly back to Mr. Alfred's plan. He knew something like this might happen to her. Oh, my, I feel as though I'd failed my trust. He trusted me to take care of her."

"Now, now, Annie, she *is* a grown woman. You can't keep treating her like a little girl. She misjudged a man and is suffering for it, but thank the good Lord she weren't harmed no more than she is. She'll get over the bruises and after a while she'll get over the heartbreak. Well, maybe she'll give thought to marryin' a man like Sir Richard who'll care for her and take pleasure in doing for her. I believe she'll be able to do that now that the earl has treated her so."

"I just wish she'd talk to me, but she won't mention him, and if I say anything about it, she turns her head and bids me leave her. I'm thinking you've the right of it when you suggested Lady Winterset. Here, John, here's your tea. I'm going this minute to Lady Winterset. The sooner said, the sooner mended."

*   *   *

The walk to Lord and Lady Winterset's townhouse took but ten minutes' brisk striding along streets on which were located homes of some of England's wealthiest families. When Annie reached the Winterset home, so great was her distress that she lost all sense of propriety and walked up the steps to the front door. It was opened by an august personage, who looked at the plainly clad woman with raised eyebrows.

"If you please," Annie said, "be so kind as to ask Lady Winterset if she would see Mrs. Carrington's Annie. It's a matter of life and death."

The butler indicated with a sniff that Annie should seat herself on a bench in the outer entryway. He left her, carefully closing the inner door, as though suspecting her designs on the *objets d'art* to be found inside the house.

"Top-lofty squeedunks, aren't ye," the woman muttered to his back. "Be proper surprised when your mistress sends for me, I've no doubt."

Annie occupied herself while she waited for Lady Winterset's summons by sorting out the words she meant to use to explain Amelia's troubles. She had no idea how much the marchioness had been told by her mistress, but what hadn't been related was going to be told this day.

The sound of the door being unlocked broke into Annie's reverie. The butler gestured to her to follow him as he announced in a most disapproving voice, "Her ladyship will see you."

He conducted Annie up the curving marble staircase to the second floor of the house to a door at the far end of the hallway, where he stopped and tapped gently. At the sound of a voice from within, he opened it and stepped back for Annie to enter, then closed the door behind her.

"Annie, is something wrong with Mrs. Carrington?" The marchioness, her hair not yet dressed for the day and still wearing a peignoir was seated at a tambour desk.

"Oh, my lady, I didn't know what to do or who else to speak to about my Miss Melly. She's in a terrible state— won't speak with anyone, not even Perry, and he's the apple of her eye. If I try to question her, she turns her back on me, and Staunton can't get a word out of her. And we're just that worried. She only says something about going back to Padua." The tears were once again coursing down Annie's cheeks.

"Calm yourself, Annie. Take off your coat and hat and sit down on that comfortable chair." Lady Winterset rose from her seat and rang for her maid. "We'll have some tea, and you shall tell me all about your problem and Mrs. Carrington's." Gradually she soothed Amelia's devoted servant. By the time the tea tray was brought into the room and placed on the Buhl table, Annie had composed herself and was ready to tell the whole tale to her hostess.

"I am telling you a story that must never go beyond this room, my lady," she began. "No one except Staunton and I know it, and it could ruin my dear Miss Melly if ever it became known."

"Do you mean about the masked lady?" Lady Winterset felt she should set Annie's mind at rest by letting her know that Amelia had confided in her. In all likelihood it would make the telling of the rest of the story easier for the woman. "Mrs. Carrington confided in me, so you need have no fears as to my honor."

"Oh, ma'am, I meant no . . . it's just that Miss Melly means the world to me, and she's been sore hurt." Annie drew a deep, sighing breath. "I may as well get right to it. No way to tell it but straight."

Speaking with much gesture and emotion, Annie recounted to Lady Winterset the tale of Amelia's growing involvement with the Earl of Croyville. "I'd like to spit in his face, him being nobility and all, for what he done to my baby," she interjected into her story. "For he's a cruel man, as anyone with an ounce of sense can see.

"Then she came home from a drive with him a few days ago and spoke with him alone in the library. After he left I could tell she had come to some kind of decision. One minute she'd be singing and laughing, and the next she'd be sitting brooding. There was no settling her down. When I taxed her with being in love with him, she told me to mind my own business. The next morning she left before I saw her. She went riding with him—and more than riding, I'll be bound. She was gone for most of the morning, and when she came home she was like a crushed flower. He treated her cruelly, Lady Winterset; she's got bruises on her arms and shoulders and . . . and . . . she keeps crying in the middle of the night and saying nothing during the day. She won't come out of her room—won't dress, won't let me do her hair, won't let Kenton, her abigail, near her. Annie paused to wipe away the tears that had fallen to her cheeks. She looked at the marchioness to gauge the effect of her tale on Amelia's friend and saw anger and pity on her face.

"I'm afraid her heart is broken, ma'am. I only hope she doesn't die from melancholy. Me and Staunton, ma'am, we love Miss Melly as though she were our own. We've been with her since she was just a wee thing. And a sweeter, more thoughtful, more loving child there never was."

"I know, Annie, she was always the best of friends to me, and I know how good and selfless she is." Eglantine paced up and down the room a few times, her brow furrowed in thought. "I think the best way to start is for me to call on her. If she will talk to me, all to the good. If she won't, then I will have to pull her out of herself. She probably has many different feelings about whatever happened. Most likely the earl discovered who she really is and was angry at her imposture. If ever she gives me permission, I will have plenty to say to him on that point." Once more the lady rang for her maid. "My Betty shall dress me and then you and I shall return to Princess Gardens and see what we can do about helping our unhappy Amelia."

Within the hour Annie and Lady Winterset were ensconced in the Winterset carriage making the short trip to Princess Gardens. It was Lady Winterset's considered opinion that Amelia must be made to divulge the events of the fateful day. How to proceed from that point would be decided upon when Lady Winterset had determined the state of Amelia's heart and health.

Before long, Mrs. Carrington was roused from her lethargy by an insistent rap on her door. Listlessly she bade the petitioner enter, expecting Annie or some one of her household. She was reclining upon her chaise, still dressed *en négligé* although it was afternoon, with her arm raised across her eyes. The pale green and russet draperies were drawn, plunging the room into a shadowed dullness that denied the bright autumn sunlight of the outdoors.

Suddenly the room filled with that sunlight as the curtains were flung back from their post over the windows.

"Don't do that. I wish to have the drapes drawn. Annie, I gave you orders—" Amelia's voice sounded more like that of a querulous old recluse than that of a vibrant young woman. "Oh, Eglantine! How did you get here? I really don't . . . Oh, go away."

"Amelia Carrington, if I didn't know you any better, I'd say you were reveling in your tears. What happened to turn you into such a milksop, such a veritable crybaby?" Lady Winterset spoke in a most unsympathetic voice, hiding her astonishment at the change in her friend. Where a few days before Amelia had presented a glowing countenance, full of life and color, today she was pale; dark smudges beneath her lusterless eyes told of sleepless nights. Even her glorious hair hung lifeless around her shoulders. The skin was taut across her cheekbones and the roundness that had softened the bone structure of her face had melted away. She was no less lovely, but, instead of the look of vital enjoyment, she had the look of a haunted princess.

"Oh, Tina, my life is ended. I took the chance that Justin would understand, I loved him so much . . ." Amelia's voice trailed away as she began to cry.

Eglantine looked at the woebegone friend. Where was the joyous woman who had described herself as feeling like a daffodil in springtime? If Justin Farnham had brought her to this pass, he would have to answer to Lady Winterset. He may have styled himself friend of the Wintersets, but she would no longer acknowledge that friendship.

Of utmost importance, before holding Farnham to account for his actions, was the necessity to restore Amelia to her former self. She must be persuaded to reach into her own reserves and draw on the tremendous strength of spirit that Eglantine knew existed. As severe as this blow had been to her self-esteem, she must rise above the hurt.

Speaking in a soft, gentle voice, Lady Winterset urged Amelia to tell her what had happened. "We have spoken of the most intimate matters, my dear, and can have no shame between us now. It is very important that you rid yourself of your disgust with yourself and understand what has happened so that you can get over it and go on to a good life. You cannot, nay, *must* not spend another minute in such a state. So will you tell me what happened? Please?" She had taken Amelia's hands in her own and clasped them tightly, refusing to let go when Amelia tried to pull away.

For a long moment there was silence. Then from behind the strands of hair that had fallen across her face, the sorrowing young woman began to speak. She spoke in a voice without emphasis, without tone, saying one word after the other, giving as much value to "and" as she did to "kiss." There were no more tears as she spoke of the death of her love by violence. There was no hint of the ecstasy she had experienced or the agony that had been hers. The words described a set of actions in which she had been a participant, but her voice droned like a reader reading a recipe for making dough. As Eglantine listened, she was more stricken by the absence of emotion than she would have been had Amelia laughed and cried, ranted and raved in the telling of her tale.

"I feel despoiled, deluded, and defrauded by the man in whom I was ready to deposit my life's love. I have decided to go back to Padua, Tina. I need the calm and the gentle life I had there. I am not made for this frenetic activity, nor for the heartbreak it brings.

"Oh, why couldn't I have told him before, when I first wanted to? But I loved him so much. I was too greedy, Tina. I couldn't be satisfied with my memories; I wanted more. And now I have nothing except a terrible memory of his anger and his hate. Oh, how shall I forget his cruelty? I can never forgive him." Finally she turned her anguished face up to her friend's. "What shall I do, Eglantine? What shall I do?"

Tina put her arms around Amelia and held her as she

stroked her back. "I am surprised, Amelia, that you show no anger at Justin. You say you won't forgive him, but you say it without fire. Where is your anger?" Eglantine arose from the chaise and began to walk around the room, examining the beautiful *objets d'art* upon the tables. "Surely you wish to avenge yourself on this man, this cad who committed such a dastardly act upon you. That you found happiness in his arms only moments before he attacked you only makes the deed more vile. There could be no provocation strong enough to produce such an action. Do you agree with me?"

"Of course I agree with you, but what am I to do?" A hint of life came into Amelia's voice, an expression of interest.

Eglantine shrugged. "If it were I, I wouldn't let him have the satisfaction of knowing that he had wounded me so deeply. I would let him see me at my very best, laughing, dancing, flirting. Let him see what he had lost in his blind anger and careless action. Buy some new gowns and take up your life as though he had never happened. Give him the cut direct if you want, or treat him with frigid politeness. Never look directly at him when you see him. It will work well with Justin because no one has ever dared to treat him so. You need never speak to him again. Just pick up your life and show him that you are well loved, sought out, and happy." She peered at Amelia.

"I don't know if I could succeed," Amelia whispered. "My heart quakes when I think of seeing him."

"We shall do something my mother taught me to do a long time ago. We shall rehearse!"

"Rehearse? Whatever do you mean?" With each exchange Amelia became more interested and left further behind in the past, the pale, wan person Eglantine had encountered when she had first entered the chamber.

"When you have bathed and dressed and had Kenton do your hair in a most flattering style, we shall play a game. I shall be the Earl of Croyville, and you shall be you. We will pretend to be at a ball, or a dinner, and you shall practice cutting me and being unutterably polite to me. That

way, when you do come across him in the course of your
social activities, you will automatically know how to behave
without thinking about it. It makes things quite a bit easier.
My mama was very clever, you know." Lady Winterset
walked over to the bellpull and signaled for Kenton. "You
must also remember you have accepted Lady Dunmore's
invitation. It would be very unwise to absent yourself from
that party."

"Oh, I couldn't go there!" Amelia cried. "He will be
there, and I don't think . . . that wouldn't be a good idea,
I'm sure."

"My dear Amelia, allow yourself to be guided by me."
Lady Winterset nodded to Kenton, who had just entered the
room. "You have more than a week to prepare yourself.
Besides which, the house is so huge and the property so
grand, you could be there for a month and manage not to
be closer to Justin than four doors away. Kenton, Mrs.
Carrington is ready to dress. We are going for a drive this
afternoon, so make her look as pretty as possible." She
returned her attention to Amelia. "I shall return for you in
two hours exactly. It's chilly out so wear something warm.
Perhaps with that outrageous sable muff! *Au revoir!*"

Lady Winterset left the house at 52 Princess Gardens
hoping that she had pulled Amelia out of her panic; for that
was what it had been. Eglantine was a shrewd judge of
character, and she knew Amelia was made of sturdy stuff.
Once she drew her out of the shell that her panic had thrown
her into, the woman would do well. And it would certainly
be a lesson to Farnham. What a brute! However, time would
tell.

CHAPTER FIFTEEN

THE BALL IN honor of Miss Blessington's come-out was in full swing and could easily be called a crush, one of the more successful events of the fall season. Elegantly coiffed women in colorful dresses of opulent fabrics, bedecked with jewels of every description, talked or danced with tall, short, fat, thin, suave, naïve men dressed in dark-toned coats with satin breeches, silk stockings and low shoes, pristine shirts and cravats in which nestled sapphires, rubies, diamonds, or pearls. The strains of the music produced by the eight-man orchestra were almost drowned out by the almost three hundred voices that were gossiping, flirting, commiserating, whining, complaining, felicitating. Servants in pale-gray livery trimmed in silver walked smoothly back and forth within the large ballroom and promenade, passing trays of glasses filled with the finest French vintage champagne, ratafia, negus, and punch.

Outstanding in a crowd of beautiful women, Amelia Carrington stood chatting with a group of her acquaintances. She was gowned in blond lace over pale-orange *mousseline de soie*. The wide, square neckline was edged with stiffened lace that became a modified Elizabethan collar, standing high behind her delicately modeled head. Her hair was dressed in a severe fashion of braids and chignon, pulled back from her face, allowing the perfection of her brow and sparkling eyes to be seen and admired. Long blond gloves covered her arms to the edge of the slightly puffed sleeves. She looked more regal than England's queen as she stood giving her undivided attention to the elderly gentleman with whom she spoke.

It was duly noted among those to whom such things were of importance that Mrs. Carrington had not danced a single dance with the Earl of Croyville. Until very recently, the *on-dit* had been that they were making a pair of it. He had taken her driving every day or two and had danced at least three dances with her at every opportunity. She had been absent from the scene the last week or so; no one of those in the know had seen them quarreling or displaying temper toward each other. Whatever had happened had evidently occurred in private. Of course, that was the earl for you. Totally inconstant. One could expect these short, intense affairs with him. But Mrs. Carrington, well, one didn't know about her since she had only been on the scene a little over two months. Not time enough to be able to judge accurately.

What was obvious to one man was that, although Mrs. Carrington smiled and occasionally laughed, there was a hint of reserve present in her demeanor; one might even say, if one were perceptive, that it was a touch of sadness in the beautiful green eyes. Sir Richard Dyckman couldn't place his finger on it; he was aware of no particular reason for that suggestion of sorrow. All he knew was that the woman he cared to call his friend had been through some sort of crisis, for nothing else could have produced that look. And it therefore followed that in some way Lord Croyville was involved in that crisis.

Gradually Sir Richard moved through the crush of bodies toward Amelia. She had begun to stroll the perimeter of the ballroom with the gentleman with whom she was talking. Dyckman was a scant ten feet from his objective when he saw her come face to face with the earl. Farnham seemed about to speak when Mrs. Carrington turned her head slightly so that her eyes slipped past his face as though he wasn't there. She continued to respond to her companion and was soon past the earl, who stopped to watch her walking away from him. Her progress continued at the same slow gait, with no perceptible pause in speech or movement. But to Richard, so heedful of Amelia's happiness, the pain in her eyes was very apparent. The hiss of surprise that ran like a ripple through those close enough to have witnessed Mrs. Carrington administer the "cut-direct" to Lord Croyville was like an exclamation point at the end of a sentence.

It had no effect on the earl. The cool expression on his face changed not one whit. He sauntered on as though unconcerned, stopping to greet this one or that as he made his way around the room.

A short while later Lady Winterset and her friend Mrs. Carrington were to be seen chatting in a secluded corner next to a huge potted palm.

"My God, Amelia, I never thought you could be so cool. After all you've been through." Eglantine wielded her fan briskly.

"It's very easy when one's heart is like an iced stone in one's chest. I can carry on because I'm numb. There seems to be no feeling in me anymore, Eglantine. I feel so empty. Do you still advise me to attend the Dunmore house party?" A look of pleading came into Amelia's eyes. "I don't know if I am redoubtable enough to stay calm throughout a two-week stay."

"I have already explained that you won't have to be any closer to him than you are tonight. He is now aware that you have no wish to speak with him, and he, whatever his faults, is intelligent enough not to wish to precipitate a scene." Lady Winterset patted her friend's arm. "Tonight you must dance and laugh as though there were nothing on your mind beyond having an enjoyable time. I've seen Sir Richard looking at you; you could encourage him, my dear. He has several good qualities, in addition to being wealthy enough to dress you in gold and gems."

"I have no wish to engage Sir Richard's attentions under false pretenses. He deserves more from a wife than I can ever give him, and I don't know whether I wish for a husband. I've had one—a good one—who left me a respectable widow. Perhaps I shall retire to the country, Eglantine, and raise bees!" A twist of a smile touched Amelia's face.

"Raise bees! What nonsense are you talking about?" was Lady Winterset's shocked response.

A tinkle of laughter escaped from Amelia. "Well, why not? I should think they would make splendid watchdogs and serve a useful function at the same time. Why, I could bottle the honey and sell it to all my friends and acquaintances here in the city. I could be a fashionable beekeeper."

Lady Winterset looked at her friend in astonishment, then, realizing that she was being teased, began to laugh in relief. "Do you know, I thought for a moment you were suffering a brain disorder. Oh, Amelia, I *am* glad to hear you laugh again. You've been truly marvelous, and I must compliment you on remaining so composed. I know this had been an ordeal."

"If you hadn't come to me the other day, Tina, I would never found the strength to carry on. You are the best of friends, Tina; as long as you stay by me I shall be able to conduct myself with decorum, even when I want to scream."

"Come, I think it's about time I went in search of my dear husband. There are too many pretty girls here, and he has a partiality for pretty girls." Eglantine started to move away from the palm, linking arms with Amelia. "Isn't this a squeeze? Mrs. Blessington will consider herself hostess of the season for accomplishing such a smashing success. Oh, Amelia, there's Sir Richard. Let's stop and talk to him."

It was Lady Winterset's purpose to have Amelia kept so busy dancing and talking that she would have no more time to brood on the unpleasant events of the past week. The return of Amelia's sense of humor was an encouraging sign.

Although Amelia had suffered grievously at the earl's hands, Eglantine hoped that eventually all would come right. She felt in her heart that Amelia Carrington would make the perfect wife for the cool, worldly earl. The very fact that there had been such an intense reaction on his part to the knowledge that Amelia was his Lady of Mystery was an indication of the depth of his feelings for her. It was doubtful he was even aware that he had come to love the girl; bringing the two of them together was the kind of challenge that was food for Lady Winterset. As long as Amelia and Justin were both at the Dunmores', she would surely be able to bring about the hoped-for results.

CHAPTER SIXTEEN

DUNMORE CHASE WAS located in the shire of Sussex, near the town of Alfriston on the Cuckmere River. Its main hall and ramparts predated the Elizabethan period, which saw the addition of the long wings on either side of the main hall. The red brick of the mansion had weathered to a mellow rose accented by white cornerstones. The park of Dunmore Chase was a polished gem of cultivated grounds that sported a small lake. The rolling grounds were artfully landscaped with formal and informal gardens, a topiary, a small maze, and a birch wood with meandering walks to entice the romantic-minded. Bordering the cultivated area were woods of birches, oaks, and beech trees that had been left in their natural state to promote the growth of the small animals indigenous to the area.

Amelia had decided to travel the sixty miles between

London and Dunmore Chase in one day, stopping only to change horses. She had had her cook pack baskets of food for an *al fresco* picnic along the way, knowing that Perry would enjoy that more than dining in the private parlor of an inn. The country was enjoying an especially mild spell for mid-November, making such outdoor activities as enjoyable as though it were mid-September. Lady Dunmore had kept her promise and had forwarded a list of the various events that would take place during the two-week stay, a list that included sightseeing around the old town of Hastings as well as hunts, a country dance, and a more formal ball and visits to local authorities.

Staunton had had the coach ready for departure at nine that morning, and they had been smartly on their way soon after. It was now close to five in the afternoon, and they were just approaching the estate's elaborate iron gates. The vehicle swept through the gates and up the long rhododendron-lined driveway. A break in the shrubberies gave them a view of the impressive mansion, and Perry squealed at the sight of tower and crenellated roofline. "It's a castle, a castle! And look, Mama, peacocks! Oh, do you think they'll open their fans for me? Where do you think the other children are? Annie, shall you take me for a walk directly?"

"I think the child was born to look for all the answers in the universe." Annie sighed, having listened to a thousand questions from the boy since early morning. "Is there something we can give him to limit his curiosity?"

Amelia laughed at Annie's woebegone face. "Annie, love, he'll be so busy for the next two weeks you'll have a good rest. There will be so many new sights and faces, I'm sure someone else will be there to answer for you."

The coach drew up before the broad steps that led into the building. Before Staunton could jump down from his seat, two footmen had come running to open the coach door and aid the passengers in alighting. Standing at the top of the stairway were Lord and Lady Dunmore and several children of various ages. Amelia, becomingly dressed in a dove-gray traveling costume, led Perry up the stairs to be greeted by her host and hostess. The warmth of their reception and the acknowledgment of Perry by the children were all that Amelia could hope for.

Instructing the youngsters to show Perry to the nursery wing, Lady Dunmore put her arm about Amelia's waist and drew her through the doorway, chattering all the time in that unusual deep voice of hers. Her diminutive figure was attired in a challis roundgown that was barely long enough to conceal the unusual shoes with high platform soles that she affected to increase her height.

"You must be exhausted, my dear. When you wrote to tell me that you were not going to stop overnight en route, I was surprised at your fortitude. I never make the distance in less than two days. Even if the second day is only two hours on the road, I am assured of arriving well rested and in my best looks!" She laughed lightly, then said *sotto voce,* "At my age one must do everything in one's power to be sure to arrive in one's best looks."

Lady Dunmore had led Amelia into an enormous entry three stories tall, which was large enough to encompass the foyer and drawing rooms as well as the library of Amelia's home in Princess Gardens. On either side of this great space was a huge fireplace filled with burning logs. Oversized carpets in glowing colors lay in the flagstone floor, with chairs of every size, shape, and historical period upon them. On the walls were animal trophies, hunted by generations of Dunmores; standing in niches on either side of the fire-places were suits of armor.

The walls themselves were stuccoed in the Tudor manner. A magnificently carved dark wood staircase centered at the far end of the hall. Hanging from poles around the upper perimeter of the area were banners that spanned three hundred years of history. Some were tattered and faded; others were still bright and relatively whole.

Lady Dunmore whisked Amelia through this space into a cozy room that seemed small by contrast. Obviously decorated in more recent years, it was filled with furniture meant for comfort and covered with fabrics that were bright and colorful. On the large table set between the two sofas was a tray with tea things and plates of comestibles.

"If you're like I am, you will be wanting your tea more than anything in the world right now. Am I right, my dear?" Lady Dunmore gestured Amelia to a seat and nodded to Lord Dunmore to sit at her side. "There, my sweet, you may sit next to our guest for now. I may have to deprive you of her company later." She turned her attention to Amelia. "We have a very self-important guest coming to dinner later, and if she's not seated next to Buffy she thinks we're angry at her. Such a pity that she lacks intelligence, because she's rather a sweet old thing, really."

Amelia, who had not yet been given time to say more than hello, started to laugh. "My dearest Lady Dunmore, I can't imagine you having anyone who was so full of their own self-importance, not unless there's a good reason for it. Tell me, is this lady an author, or a famous explorer, or perhaps an even more famous relative?"

"Haw! She's caught you out!" Lord Dunmore guffawed.

"You are too clever, Amelia. You're right about a relative. She's an elderly maiden aunt of Buffy's, and if she doesn't sit next to him—well!" Lady Dunmore handed Amelia a cup of tea. "You know, you really must stop lording and ladying us. It's about time we were on first-name basis. It would be so much friendlier that way, I'm sure. So you will call me Bella, and you will call him"— she waved her hand at her husband—"Buffy. Silly name. Don't even remember where it came from, but he's a love, in spite of it."

"Thank you, Bella. I should like that above all things." Amelia sipped her tea, then accepted a cake from Lord Dunmore. "This is a vast home. Do you ever lose yourselves? I swear I would. I just hope I don't lose Perry here!"

"No chance of that." Lady Dunmore slapped her husband's hand as he reached for his third cake. "Now, Buffy, you know what the doctor said. Not more than one and you've already had two. If you want to enjoy the sweet table tonight, you'd better save yourself. What were we talking about? Oh, yes, this barn of a place. It's very nice to have a home of historical significance, but it is quite difficult to keep up with the repairs. Sometimes I wonder if we wouldn't be better off just tearing the whole thing down and building a nice little box of a house. The only problem is, where would we hold our entertainments?"

Lady Dunmore continued to conjecture on various types of hypothetical homes, then said, "Buffy, my dear, wouldn't you like to take a nap before it's time to dress for dinner? You mentioned being tired before." She gave a peculiar movement with her head to signal that she wanted to be alone with Amelia. "There's a good boy. You'll feel much more the thing after you've rested."

Lord Dunmore, who obviously understood his wife's sign language, walked over to Amelia and in his soft voice expressed the hope that she would enjoy her stay at the chase. "And I'm lookin' forward to havin' you at my side at the dinner table. Bella knows I like to talk to a pretty woman. I'll be on my way now. Take good care of her, Bella. She seems like a good gel."

Amelia stifled the laughter that bubbled up in her throat. That was undoubtedly the longest statement she had heard her host utter.

"That Buffy—he's nothing if not obvious, but then, you must expect men to appreciate you, beautiful as you are." Lady Dunmore patted Amelia's hand reassuringly. "You know, Amelia, I believe in plain speaking, no roundaboutation. You must understand Buffy and I are concerned about you. I look upon myself almost like your dear mother." The worthy lady paused for breath. "You were out of the country for several years and may have forgotten, dear child, how important it is for one as young as yourself to be married. You are not yet old enough to remain a widow without becoming an 'item,' no matter how circumspect your life. If you marry, you can have more children and look forward to a full and happy life." Lady Dunmore didn't wait for an answer. "There are several eligible men to whom you will be introduced during your stay here, and, of course, Justin Farnham will be present."

Amelia withdrew her hand from under Lady Dunmore's. "Dear Bella, you are everything wonderful, and you must believe I appreciate your concern on my behalf. But do please let us forget matchmaking for this visit." She laughed lightly, trying to control the quiver of anger at the sound of Farnham's name. "I should like to forget all that for several days, so please allow me the luxury of ignoring the necessity of finding a husband. At least while I am your guest."

"Darling gel, of course *you* may ignore it, but I doubt the gentlemen will. Your beauty and intelligence are like nectar to a bee. But there, I'm sure Justin will attend to keeping you away from the other pursuers."

"You mistake Lord Croyville's interest, ma'am. He has no call to occupy himself with my affairs in any way at all." Suddenly agitated, Amelia rose from the sofa and walked to the window, presenting her back to Lady Dunmore. "I have no wish to seek out his solicitude and ask you, with all due respect, not to take issue with me on this matter."

Amelia's unexpected vehemence silenced Lady Dunmore. One could not call my lady insensitive exactly; rather she could be said to have a singular sense of purpose that blinded her to an individual's wishes. In the case of Amelia and Justin, Lady Dunmore had decided that they would make a suitable partnership, especially since she had been witness to their partiality for each other.

"Of course you don't wish to seek out his interest, my dear, but I saw his eyes when he looked at you that day in your library. The man is besotted, no matter how coolly he tries to act. And you are in like case. I saw you return his glance."

Amelia turned to face Lady Dunmore. "My lady, whatever you may think you saw, there is and will be nothing between Lord Croyville and myself. He is notorious for giving and withdrawing his interest more often than you or I would . . . would . . . oh, change our hats. I assure you that the falling off of his attention has been in the natural course of events. Undoubtedly a newer face on the scene has caught his roving eye. Please, deny yourself the disappointment that would necessarily be yours if you pursue the dream of uniting Lord Croyville and myself. It is an impossible one."

The younger woman returned to her seat, forcing herself

to calmness. She poured another cup of tea for herself and offered some to her hostess. When finally she spoke again, she asked what plans were in course for the morrow. Lady Dunmore, deciding for once that discretion was the better part of valor, responded by describing a sightseeing trip and picnic planned to Battle Abbey, near Hastings, and to the ruins of Hastings Castle. The party would lunch on the mount, where they would have a good view of the coastline.

After several minutes of talk about the plans for the drive, Amelia was relieved to hear Lady Dunmore suggest a short rest before dressing for dinner. The lady herself conducted Amelia to her chamber, where at long last the young woman was able to let herself respond to the thought of Justin Farnham. Only in solitude could she mourn the "might have been."

Blind to the splendors of the room in which she was to reside for the next two weeks, Amelia paced the cream-colored Turkey carpet, unconsciously shaping her walk to the pattern of the design. The shell-pink hangings cast a soft roseate light that warmed the room but not Amelia's loneliness. Her confusion at the ambivalence of her feelings about Farnham kept her in turmoil. As she strode back and forth, she exhorted herself to be strong, to close her eyes to the qualities in her former lover that she had found so endearing. She adjured herself to think only of the harshness with which he had used her. She told herself that in truth he was a mere philanderer and would undoubtedly have used her and then thrown her away in any case.

At long last she threw herself across her bed, admitting in her heart of hearts that no matter what he had done she would always love him. The fury she had felt after that appalling afternoon in the little house had changed. When Amelia examined the incident with complete honesty, she realized that Justin's actions had probably been triggered by jealousy. He as much as said he had loved his mysterious lady, and upon realizing that she and Amelia were one and the same, had responded to the revelation with a welcome. As he spoke, the welcome had changed to virulence; in his mind he had tried and convicted her of being a wife who had cuckolded her husband. The Farnham pride prevented his being able to accept her explanation for seeking out a lover. She had heard that his own mother had had several lovers without hiding her affairs from her husband or her son. It was no wonder that Justin was so filled with cynicism about women. That cynicism was his shield against the possibility of ending as his father had—withdrawn, bitter, and ineffectual.

Despite her understanding of the earl's character, Amelia could not face her own responses to his attack on her. That she had reacted to his assault with an even greater tempest of passion shocked her. How could she lose control of herself like that? His fury had excited her beyond the limits to which his skill had at first taken her. It was true that he had not really been cruel once he had started to caress her body . . . furious yes, but not actually brutal. But still . . . she had not wanted him to touch her once he had shown his anger and she had tried to fight him off. How then could she have given in so easily? She must speak further with Eglantine. If she were ever again to contemplate a physical union with a man, she must understand herself or she could too easily become a slave to her body.

Just to think about the earl kindled the ever-ready flame; her mouth moved as though to his kiss, her arms strained to enfold him, her breasts readied for the touch of his hand.

Tears running down her cheeks, Amelia finally fell asleep, whispering Justin's name as though to call him to her side.

CHAPTER SEVENTEEN

THE CLEAR, CRISP air of late November carried the sound of moving vehicles. A parade of three open carriages, each carrying several people of various ages and accompanied by mounted riders, drew up beside the crumbling walls of Hastings Castle. Amid much laughter and calling back and forth, passengers and riders dismounted and disembarked, eager to indulge in the magnificent feast laid out under an ancient copper beech tree. A long table, covered with crisp white cloths, had been put into service as the repository for the sumptuous repast. Dishes of sliced ham, delicately pink; platters of poultry *en gelée,* decorated with slices of orange and whole mushrooms; salmon, served whole, poached and covered with *crème mayonnaise;* bowls of fresh vegetables from the estate succession houses; a bowl of fruit and flowers; trays of pickles and relishes—all beckoned to the hungry sightseers.

Heavy wool blankets piled with pillows were spread around, creating informal seating for the guests; each blanket was complete with a few tiny stands·on which the diners could desposit their wine glasses. Liveried footmen moved about serving the food and drink.

"Lady Dunmore, this is a delight. With what magic did you create such a banquet?" Lady Winterset stood with her hostess to one side of the scene, nodding and smiling as various friends beckoned her to join them.

"The magic of a marvelous chef and a superior butler! That's all it takes." Lady Dunmore took a glass of wine from the tray proffered by one of the footmen. "Will you look at that silly Mary Semple. She's all agog over young Sir Edwin Bristone and hasn't enough sense to hold herself just a tiny bit more aloof than she is. Keeps putting herself in his way, pushes him to take flight. Excuse mc while I send young Chiswick over to distract her." Lady Dunmore sped off to do her duty as a hostess, leaving Eglantine to wander over to her husband.

"Hallo, George. How was the ride over?" she asked the slim, fair-haired man. "Anything of interest to tell me? It was too funny in the carriage. Miss Cordwainer and Lady Olivia were in alt over being in a gathering with the exalted J. Farnham. They were each describing to the other how they were going to attract his attention. Pah . . . to think a seventeen-year-old would attract a man as worldly as Justin."

"He may be worldly, my sweet, but he is also very weary. Something has happened to him recently that has sent him into a regular melancholy. Very unlike him." Lord Winterset pondered his friend's humors for a moment, eyeing his wife. "Eglantine, you have a look on your face that tells me you know something of the matter. What troubles my friend? Tell me!"

"My dear husband and best of friends"—Eglantine moved to her husband's side and put her arm through his—"I have a suspicion, but I can't share it with you without permission from someone else. Dear heart, if you think about our friend's activities this past few weeks, you may be able to solve the puzzle." The elegant woman leaned against her spouse. "I shall tell you this though. If it is in my power to do so, I shall have Lord Croyville building castles in the air before long."

Lord Winterset held his wife at arm's length as he studied her. "Are you up to some mischief, my lady love? Why do I always get the feeling that you're leaving me behind with your machinations?" He pulled her into the curve of his arm. "Just don't let yourself be hurt. You sometimes forget that the people don't always wish to play the game your way."

Lady Winterset stood with her husband awhile longer, enjoying his company. She watched approvingly as Amelia laughed and flirted mildly with two gentlemen. She was not as approving when she saw Sir Richard approach her friend and engage her in conversation, gradually moving Amelia away from the two potential suitors. The baronet's quiet dignity and self-possession was shield enough against the highspirited nonsense that was going on among the younger members of the party. Eglantine watched him guide Amelia toward the ruins, wishing that she could overhear their conversation.

This was the first time in more than a week that Sir Richard had spent any time with Amelia. He had been in Leicestershire tending to his estates and had been out of touch with her for the past days. When he had taken his leave of her, he had remarked on her spirits and ease of manner. Upon meeting with her this day, he had wondered at the change in her. She was quieter, not withdrawn but not completely a part of the company. Her lustrous green eyes still held a shadow of sadness that he could not understand.

"Have you quite finished examining me, Sir Richard?" the lady asked unexpectedly. "I believe you will be able to exactly detail every wrinkle in my face, should you desire to."

"Not so, Amelia. I was merely comparing you with my memory of last week. It seems to me something must have happened that has blue deviled you. Is there something I can do to make things right for you? It would be my pleasure."

"I think it must be too much entertaining, Sir Richard. I'm not accustomed to late nights and early days. Our life was quite quiet in Padua." Amelia sat down on the broken wall to watch the children play.

"This scene reminds me of our shipboard days, a merry company come together to share food, drink, and laughter. Is that all it is, too much fun and frivolity? You would tell me if something was troubling you, wouldn't you?" Sir Richard sat down nearby. "It's not your son, is it?"

"No, not at all. You can see he plays with the other children without a care in the world. They are certainly enjoying this historic spot, albeit for the wrong reasons. Look at them, running and jumping like mountain goats. I wonder if they see the same things we see or if their vision is enchanced in some way so they see a magical place that's hidden from us." Amelia removed her *bergère* bonnet and played with the ribbons as she spoke. "I remember when I was a child, I never recognized the places I'd been to from my parents' descriptions. What to them was a meadow to me might be a ballroom or a battlefield; a hole in the hedge was a cave, a tunnel, or even a coach. Do all children imagine like that, do you suppose?"

"Of a certainty," the baronet replied. "I recall a ship I captained when I was young, a great vessel with three masts and the finest linen sails. My crew was the boldest and I the bravest captain. When I was fifteen my ship turned into a huge pile of boulders that had been excavated when my father built a folly on our great lawn. I never was able to recapture the wonder of that ship again. I would say that we reach adulthood when we lose our fondest fantasy."

"You are very comforting to talk to, Sir Richard." Amelia smiled at her escort.

"I shall be more than happy to give you my help—in anything, Amelia." Sir Richard lifted himself from the crumbled wall. "In fact, I would like to—"

"Richard, I value your friendship very much." Amelia quickly put her hand up to stop Sir Richard. "Please don't ask me for that which I can't give you. Not yet."

"As long as you phrase it that way, I will still have hope that you will allow me to finish my question one day." Sensing Amelia's distress, Sir Richard laughed lightly. "I shall soon begin to make a count of the unfinished questions I have begun to try to get answered, my dear."

On the opposite side of the ruins Lord Croyville stood alone in the shadow of a large yew. He had watched the colloquy between Amelia and Sir Richard, and had been inexplicably angered by the baronet. His thoughts went back to that distressing morning when he had discovered Amelia and his lady Mystère to be one and the same. The explosion of rage had shocked him even as he had taken the beautiful woman so cruelly. The sight of the birthmark that discolored the creamy satin of the underside of her breast had at first filled him with joy. Then the joy had turned to a storm of hatred when he construed her behavior as betrayal—first of her husband and then of him. He had taken her then as harshly as he could, to erase the humiliation he felt himself to have suffered at her hands. In the aftermath of that debacle he had been scored by the whip of her venom when she threw the word "son" at him. He could hardly believe that the charming child he had saved from injury that day in the park was his son. In all likelihood she was striking out at random, trying to hurt him as he evidently had hurt her.

The earl's eyes were drawn to the children as they played battle along the tumbled walls of the castle. Perry had tied one of the large serviettes around his neck so that it hung like a cape from his shoulders. He was wielding a small branch, stripped of leaves, as though it were a sword. His shrill voice sang out commands to his followers as he lunged and parried with the invisible opponents. As he chopped and jumped about, his dark eyes flashing, he assumed the stance of victor, sword held high, one foot elevated, resting on the upthrust rock.

Justin blinked at the picture the child presented. It was in just such a stance that the artist had captured his grandfather in the portrait that hung in the gallery at Croyville. The resemblance was astonishing. The elder Farnham had been painted as St. George, victorious after slaying the dragon, and had been a young man when the portrait was painted. The same exultant look that had been preserved in paint was on the face of Peregrine Carrington. Amelia had told him the truth then when in her fury she had spat that information at him.

At the same moment that Farnham accepted the idea that Perry was his natural son, he was stabbed with a feeling of joy such as he had never known. He was a father; not only that, but the father of a bright, intrepid boy whose lineage announced itself to the knowing eye.

"You've finally recognized him, haven't you?" The soft voice of Eglantine Winterset came from in back of his left shoulder. "He's exactly as you must have been at the same age, Justin."

"Then you know. He looks like my grandfather did as a boy." The earl's words were slow; no trace of the proud Croyville could be heard. "I didn't really believe Amelia when she told me. I thought she lied in an attempt to wound me. How could she have done what she did? I loved her, Eglantine, all those years ago. And I never had a chance to tell her."

"Do you know her story, Justin?" The marchioness pulled Farnham's arm until he turned around.

"Not really. I didn't hear what she said. I was in such a state of anger at the time."

"She was very young when her father died, and all alone in the world—no money, no relatives, only Alfred Carrington, who had been a friend of her father's." Lady Winterset began Amelia's story. "I met her when we were about twelve years old and new to boarding school. She was the quiet one, but a real Trojan; brave as they come and true as a trump. She was seventeen when Alfred married her, and she was eternally grateful to that good, generous man for saving her from God knows what kind of a life. She had loved him as a child loves a favorite uncle. Then she added to that love gratitude, and respect.

"Alfred very much wanted children, and there were none. Amelia went to doctors, witches, gypsies, and whoever held out some hope. Finally, after five years, she decided the only way was to find a . . . a surrogate father. She chose very carefully, not to please herself but to give her child the qualities that seemed to be desirable."

Eglantine stopped for a moment as though expecting a remark from Farnham. He was once again watching his son at play and offered no comment. She continued: "She chose after much careful thought; she chose you. If I had known, I would have told her to run in the other direction, but I had been out of contact with her since her father had died. To her consternation, she found herself falling in love with you. You were young, handsome, exciting, and experienced—very different from anyone she had known until then and certainly different from the only man she had been to bed with. She wrestled with the angel, Justin; she made the choice between honoring her husband or following her heart. She chose honor. The rest you know. Alfred, as far as she knows, never realized Perry was another man's child. He died, grateful and happy. Amelia never expected to see you again. When she did, she fought her love, recognizing your attitude about marriage.

"But she loved you so much, she had decided to tell you the whole story. If you offered to make her your mistress after that, she was prepared to accept you. She's too good for you, Justin. You would have to change tremendously to deserve her. I don't know whether you want to or whether you're able to." Eglantine fell silent.

The earl stood still, unable to respond to Eglantine for the pain in his heart. He thought of Amelia's strength. For the first time in his life Lord Croyville felt ashamed of his actions. He, who had always treated women with a disdainful courtesy, thinking them to be less than men in their feelings, had been shown true courage and sacrifice. How he could have likened Amelia to his mother for one second? His mother had been a selfish, pleasure-ruled woman who had given no thought to her husband or her son in her search to satiate her appetites. He had determined that never would he suffer as his father had; never would he allow a woman to have such power to wound him. He had guarded himself so carefully that when a truly honorable woman came his way, one to whom he might easily have given his heart, he chose to judge her blindly.

Unable to face Eglantine, he kept his eyes on his son. "I never thought to feel such pain at any actions I had taken. If it were possible to do over what I have done so poorly, I would not hesitate to make repairs. But it can't be and I—I am not sure what to do now. I know I want to talk to the boy. I wish to engage him in conversation and tell him stories and teach him to ride and . . . I wish to be his father. But I have no right . . . not after what has happened between Amelia and myself."

Triumph shone in Lady Winterset's eyes. She had been sure the earl had strong feelings for her friend; hearing him speak in such a manner verified her opinion. "You have exhibited a rather infantile side of yourself, Justin. Temper tantrums never helped anyone gain friends. It may be, though, that you haven't altogether lost the lady. You shall have to move slowly with her, but then I told you that when you first met her, didn't I? What do you wish of her? Will you make her your countess, or will you hide her away in a little house somewhere?" Lady Winterset refused to dissemble.

The earl finally faced Eglantine, raising his eyebrows at her questions. "My dear Eglantine, aren't you rushing your fences? She will, in all likelihood, not even speak to me, much the less allow me to make her an offer."

"I like to know what the future will bring. Now, that's not rushing things, is it? After all, if I'm to help you mend *your* fences, I must know what's about." Lady Winterset allowed herself to smile at Farnham. "I do have a plan, which I shall disclose to you when I have thought it out a bit more. In the meantime I would caution you to be your most polite. Be conciliatory without being effusive. You may nod at the lady when she is with someone, and if you can contrive to get close enough to her when she is alone, you may wish her a pleasant evening. Don't try to overwhelm her with your contrition. It won't do to undercut yourself by expounding on your guilt. You may lavish attention upon Perry, though. Let the lady see that you are impressed with your son. In this roundabout way, she will begin to guess that you accept her. Now remember, no more than two or three words at most to Amelia, no matter how much else you wish to say. Do you promise to obey me in this?"

The earl smiled reluctantly. "I can see no other way to attain my goal, witch. You always were a schemer. Yes, I promise to listen and follow your every instruction. After all, you are a woman and should know better than I how to win a reluctant woman's heart."

"I don't think she's that reluctant, but she may prove difficult because you have treated her abominably."

CHAPTER EIGHTEEN

THE FIRST HUNT was over and the participants were cele-
brating over a sumptuous dinner prepared by the Dunmores'
temporary French chef. The dining room was aglitter with
the light of hundreds of candles, which reflected from silver
utensils, sparkling crystal goblets, and gleaming Coleport
china. Bowls of beautifully arranged flowers were spaced
down the length of the table. Footmen quietly offered platters of exotic viands to the guests, then later, directed by
the wine steward, poured the wines.

Coming from the far end of the table, the sound of hearty
laughter broke through the softer sounds of conversation.
Lord Dunmore leaned toward Amelia, seated to his right
beside Mr. Spence-Grey. Opposite Amelia, Lady Winterset
was giving her astringent opinion of strong, intrepid hunters
who, mounted on fiery steeds and following a ravening pack

of hounds, chased after a single, inoffensive animal whose only sin was to have been born a fox.

"Now, can you find anything in your experience that gives worse odds than those allowed the poor fox? It's sinful, and when one thinks that this...game...is beloved of Englishmen—well! So much for honor, say I." Lady Winterset looked down her aristocratic nose in mock disapproval.

"I say, Lady Winterset, when you describe the hunt like that, I do begin to wonder." Lord St. Aldrich, seated on Eglantine's left, sipped his wine before adding, "However, if we were on foot, the fox might bite back!"

"Enough, enough. My sides ache from laughing," Lord Dunmore exclaimed. "Tomorrow, when we go out again, you can put your advice to practice. Then we may all judge who has the right of it."

At the other end of the table, Lady Dunmore remarked to Lord Croyville that Mrs. Carrington was in exceedingly good looks tonight. She noted the somewhat distracted attitude my lord had displayed this evening. He seemed to be concerned with the events at Lord Dunmore's end of the table.

"Who is this Mr. Spence-Grey, Bella? I don't recall meeting him before" was his response to the comment about Mrs. Carrington.

"No wonder. He's several years your junior and has been with the army these past four years. He's just returned from France, made quite a name for himself over there. I believe Amelia is quite taken with him."

If Lady Dunmore had used a knife instead of words, the results could not have been more painful to Lord Croyville. "It's about time she was thinking of taking a husband. I was sure she would accept Sir Richard—he seems to have lost his head to her completely—but she regards him more as a friend, even a brother, which could be a good beginning for a marriage. Less strain on the nerves and fewer arguments if the parties are friends. Don't you agree, Justin?" She looked at him with sly eyes.

"Sir Richard...yes, I had wondered about that. He's a fine man, but too settled for Mrs. Carrington, I should think.

Tell me, Bella, what wicked thoughts are in your head? I sense a mischief. Are you so bored that you are trying to prick me with your inuendoes?" Justin smiled at Lady Dunmore. "I'm alert to you, madam. You don't have to hit me with a hammer to awaken me to the obvious."

"I just wanted to be sure of the direction you were taking, Justin. She's quite a gel. Wouldn't like to see her hurt." Lady Dunmore patted the earl's hand. "Now, let's talk of other things. How is your dear Aunt Emily? Have you seen her lately?"

Justin allowed himself to be distracted by Lady Dunmore's questions. She had surprised him with her warning about Amelia; he hadn't known his interest was so obvious. He must avoid showing his partiality—this time not for the same reasons as in the past. He would follow Eglantine's advice; polite acknowledgment of Amelia's presence and active involvement with his son.

His son. A wave of emotion swept over Justin, surprising him. His need for this small male offspring hit him like a bolt out of the blue. He had admired the child's bravery when his pony had run away with him, but never had he experienced such a profound sensation as when he knew that the boy was his son. He knew now that it was partly because of his feelings for Amelia. Finally he allowed himself to acknowledge his love for her.

Deep in thought, the earl was unaware of being the focus of inquiring glances. His shapely hand slowly twirled his wine glass. Finally he woke from his study when Lady Dunmore poked him with her fan.

"Justin, the ladies are retiring to the drawing room. It's time for you to recall yourself to the living. Miss Foulkes would like to have you attend her after you take your port. And Mrs. Livesey and her husband wish to renew their acquaintance with you. You are here for the sociability of the occasion, are you not?" Lady Dunmore rose, signaling the ladies that it was time to leave the men to their cigars and talk. "Don't be too long." were her parting words.

Amelia, arm in arm with Eglantine, left the room in Lady Dunmore's wake. But when the men joined them later, the beautiful young woman could not help but be aware of the earl's gaze. Nor could she control the quiver that went through her body when her glance met his. She refused to allow herself to respond. She would not again permit him to disrupt her life as he had. So she laughed and chatted and engaged in a light flirtation with her dinner partners. Somehow she managed to get through the evening without betraying her agitation. To anyone watching her, she seemed to be having a most enjoyable time. Her honey-colored head nodded and trembled with laughter; her slender figure, in a deep-cinnamon velvet gown, moved gracefully as she strolled the room with first one and then the other of her admirers. She fluttered her fan, twinkled her eyes, and behaved like a woman being courted by the cream of the *ton,* showing appreciation for the courtship without committing herself to any.

Never once did she betray her perturbation over the searching looks coming her way from the earl. He had taken a stance near the window and was leaning negligently against the wall, watching her. It took almost all her strength to keep from running from the salon to the sanctuary of her bedchamber.

When finally Lady Dunmore arranged several tables of whist and ordered the earl to play as Amelia's partner, Amelia refused on the pretext that she cared less for the game than did Lady Abinton, who was an avid card player. She wandered over to the piano and sat down to play softly for a while. he evening seemed interminable, despite the efforts of her courtiers to engage her interest, and it was with relief that she finally excused herself.

In the safety of her room, she was able to let the tears fall. "I know he is going to try to take Perry away from me. I can just see it in his eyes. He keeps studying me." She wept into her pillow for a few moments, then calmed down, her sobs dwindling away as a child's into occasional deep shudders. She lay on the bed, curled about the huge pillow clutched in her arms for comfort. It was impossible to put Justin Farnham from her mind.

The following morning, those guests intent upon joining

the hunt gathered in the courtyard. Perry had been watching the excitement from the terrace, dressed in his riding clothes, hoping to go with the grown-ups. Before mounting her cream-colored horse, Amelia stopped to kiss him good-bye and caution him to behave himself while she was absent. To her surprise, the boy asked permission to accept Lord Croyville's invitation to ride with him.

"Perry dearest, are you sure the earl asked you to go riding with him? Perhaps he was just funning."

"Oh, no, Mama, he even said we would take a path away from the hunt so that my pony wouldn't get too excited by all the hullabaloo." The child wrinkled his brow. "My lord said he would like to get to know me better. He said I remind him of his grandfather who was a very . . . trepid . . . or something like that, man. What did he mean?"

Rather taken aback by the comparison, Amelia answered, "I believe he meant to say you're very brave. All right, Perry. You may go with the earl, but be on your best behavior. And no galloping."

Upon receiving his word to be well behaved, Amelia left to mount and join the group of lively riders. She kept glancing back toward the terrace until she saw the earl's tall figure join Perry. A mist seemed to blur their two figures as she watched, and she dashed her gloved hand over her eyes. By then they were walking toward the stables, the tall man bent slightly to the side as though listening to the child, whose eager face was upturned.

At some point during the morning's chase, Amelia lost any interest she might have felt for the hunt. By then she had been outdistanced by the field and was riding alone with her thoughts. Curious about her son's day with his father, she returned to the hall in hopes of speaking with Perry. To her consternation, the father and son had not yet returned to the mansion. She admitted she was behaving like a lamenting Niobe without cause and tried to settle down with a book in the comfortable library. But she sat staring at the words on the page, seeing only Perry and his father. A storm of fury swept over her. How dare he try to take the child from her. Where was he when she needed him? How dare he show his face where she was present after the way he treated her! How *dare* he? She jumped up, spilling the book to the floor, enraged at the arrogance of the man. To so blatantly try to win *her* son.

The sound of the book's dull thud as it hit the carpet recalled her to herself. She must be losing her mind. He *was* the boy's father. She had left him and never told him so until that day. Did she have the right to keep Perry from him? She really must try to find it in her heart to be generous with the child. Only *he* must promise never to tell Perry. Maybe he would try to turn Perry against her. No, she was being irrational. There was no reason for him to do that; except that he hated her, she knew he did. Oh, God, what should she do? And so her mood changed from anger to despair to reason.

At long last Amelia heard her son's voice in the hall. She opened the library door to find herself face to face with the earl. His dark eyes were crinkled in a smile at the upturned face of the child, who was profusely thanking Farnham for a "bestest" day.

"Oh, Perry, I'm glad you're back." Amelia could think of nothing else to say.

"Oh, Mama, we had such a good time. Lord Croyville had me up on his horse just so I should know how much different it is from so high up, and we saw a baby rabbit, and he's going to take me fishing in the stream, and we saw a falcon and seven squirrels, and I even threw them some acorns and—"

Lord Croyville interrupted his son. "Perry, if you wait until you can sit down with your mother, I'm sure she will enjoy hearing about your adventures this afternoon." He turned to Amelia with a small bow. "You have a charming son, Mrs. Carrington; it's been a pleasure to be with him. Thank you." Then, bidding Perry to mind his manners, he betook himself to his chambers.

Amelia was astonished at his abrupt leavetaking. During the rest of the day her mind whirled with confused thoughts and feelings concerning the earl, and that night she found it difficult to sleep.

CHAPTER NINETEEN

As THOUGH IN keeping with Amelia's mood, the next few days were gray and rainy, too wet for the fox hunting to continue. Lady Dunmore was able to keep her guests occupied with pantomimes, charades, and a group of children's games that no one had played since they had been tots. The sophisticated members of the *ton* would never have believed that they could make the chase echo with the sounds of their laughter as they played hide and seek, fox and hounds, spillikins, and other such diversions. Lord Croyville could usually be seen in company with young Perry. To Amelia's distress, the boy was fast growing fond of the tall, dark man who seemed to be such a fine playmate. The earl not only found amusement in keeping him company, but he also organized the Dunmore grandchildren into a brigade of soldiers, a search party looking for a lost princess, and a group of explorers making their way through the deepest jungles of Africa.

When his friends thought about his strange conduct at all, they put it down to boredom, then continued to enjoy their hostess's entertainments.

If Amelia had listened to some of the conversations between Perry and the earl, she would have been surprised at their content. One discussion concerned the need of a young gentleman for a father. Perry argued very reasonably that boys needed a man to show them the ways of the world. After all, he contended, women didn't know about things like duels, guns, and soldiering. It took a man to understand such subjects. His mother was a great gun. She rode like the wind and never scolded him when he chose more exciting pastimes than sitting with Annie or playing skittles with one of the maids. But from certain glances Perry threw his way, the earl gathered the unspoken suggestion that he would be seriously considered as a potential father. Knowing that he had his son's approval encouraged Farnham. Unfortunately, Amelia had not yet been consulted as to her feelings on the matter.

Eventually the weather changed, to the delight of the visitors to Dunmore Chase. A day was allowed for the grounds to dry out, and the next fox hunt was announced at dinner that evening.

"I can't believe my ears," Lady Dunmore scolded her guests. "I don't believe you've enjoyed my company at all, and here I went to such great lengths to entertain you. I see now you've really come just for the riding. Perhaps you'll all fall in the mud, and I shall have my vengeance!"

"Really, Bella! You know you love the hunt as much as we do. It's the only time we ladies are permitted to ride to the wind. Otherwise we must be so...ladylike!" Lady Winterset laughed at her hostess. "We all need the exercise after the gigantic feasts you've been feeding us. We shall turn into butterballs if we continue like this."

"Very well, it shall be bread and water and take your fences as you will!" the marchioness replied. "We'll have an early start in the morning. You're all so eager, I wouldn't want to delay the chase."

As the company moved about, forming smaller groups for conversation, Lady Dunmore approached Justin. "Are you planning to join us tomorrow?" she asked.

"Of course, why do you ask?"

"We've seen so little of you these past few days. You seem to have found the company of the children much more stimulating than ours."

"Everyone needs a change of pace. They're clever little monsters. Their minds aren't clouded with the exigencies of the *ton*. Rather refreshing really." The earl smiled at Lady Dunmore. "I think I've been too bored the past years to realize that there's another way of thinking."

"And what shall you do to alleviate your boredom?" the lady asked.

"It's not inconceivable that I may do something really drastic. I may even marry." The earl fingered his quizzing glass. "If I can convince the lady in question to have me," he added quietly.

Lady Dunmore felt a quick surge of sympathy for the dashing nobleman. She had never before heard him speak with uncertainty about anything. It was clear he had finally accepted his love for Amelia and was ready to make her his wife; whether she would acquiesce in his decision was a moot point.

"Dear Justin, if I didn't love you so well, I could almost relish your anxiety. It's not often one sees you at a loss. I presume you're speaking of Amelia?" Lady Dunmore felt privileged to be direct, having known the earl since he had been a child. "She doesn't seem to be desirous of your company; in fact, she has been enjoying quite some popularity. I would imagine she'll receive several offers before the week is out. Sir Richard we all know about, but now she seems to have captivated Barton Spence-Grey as well as St. Aldrich. She certainly is a very popular young woman."

"I never thought I'd ever be admitting to being at my wit's end, Bella, but I am. She seems not to want to hold even the smallest conversation with me. I compliment her on her boy, and she merely says 'thank you' and walks away. I mention the weather, and she shrugs and walks away. I offer her tea, and she declines and walks away." Justin sighed and grimaced. "It's difficult, to say the least, to court a lady who is forever walking away."

"Perhaps tomorrow, when you're out in the field, you can ride next to her; make your presence known to her in all situations, without demanding any response from her. She'll gradually take you for granted." Lady Dunmore searched for words to encourage Farnham. "I truly believe she is coming about. Occasionally, when you are with Perry she watches you with something that might almost be termed approval. She dotes on the boy, you know; I think that if you continue courting him, you may win her. In any case, if I can put in a good word for you, be assured I will."

Soon after Lord Croyville's conversation with Lady Dunmore, the party broke up for the evening, all present wishing to be at their best for the next day's activities.

After a somewhat restless night, Amelia woke to the smell of coffee being served by Annie. The curtains had already been drawn back from the mullioned windows and the early-morning sun was pouring in through the small panes.

"Good morning, lovey," Annie greeted the young woman. "It's a beautiful day out, just fine for the hunters, although the fox may not like it so well. Now, get yourself up and eat your breakfast. I wouldn't want you to faint from hunger on top of that great beast of a horse of yours." She held out the soft wool challis robe for Amelia. "Here you go, just wrap yourself in this and sit yourself at the table over here. That's a good girl."

"Annie! Stop talking to me as though I were still thirteen. I'm almost thirty, for heaven's sake." Amelia tied the sash of the robe. "Is anyone downstairs yet?"

Annie assured her mistress that none of the guests had descended but that Staunton had already saddled her horse and was awaiting her appearance.

By the time Amelia appeared on the terrace, most of the other guests had arrived and greeted the master of the hunt. The crisp, clear air seemed to make sounds sharper, colors brighter. Eglantine and George were exchanging bets with St. Aldrich as Justin looked on. Before Amelia changed the focus of her attention, his eye caught hers in a long exchange. To her amazement, a wide smile brightened his lean face as he mouthed "good morning" at her. Then, as quickly as the smile appeared, it disappeared, and she wasn't quite sure she had seen it at all. For the first time in days, she felt more like herself.

Amelia allowed Staunton to assist her in mounting, then she guided her horse over to the hunt master to ask the direction of the course. The scarlet-coated Mr. Asprey, mounted on a spirited chestnut gelding, greeted her with flattering attention.

The sharp barks of the hounds, the shouts of the packmaster, and the excited laughter of the riders all infused the morning with a sense of expectation. Amelia could feel the ebullition of the crowd affecting her horse as well as herself. A tremor of anticipation seemed to run through horse and rider as they awaited the sound of the horn. She leaned forward to run her gloved hand over the animal's neck, reassuring him. As she stroked him, she examined the crowd. The women, mounted sidesaddle, were dressed in habits of all styles and colors. Amelia had worn her black-velvet habit with a simple white stock and feather-adorned top hat. The men, looking equally fashionable, wore coats of dark superfine or broadcloth in claret, brown, blue, or green. Some of the more dandified had large pearl or silver buttons adorning their jackets.

Visible even in that well-dressed and mounted crowd, the Earl of Croyville sat astride his horse, a mote of calm in the shifting, restless assemblage. His dark gaze rested upon Amelia. She watched in fascination as his eyebrow twitched upward to be followed by a courteous lowering of his head in recognition of her notice. At this second greeting, a slow blush crept up her neck to cover her face. For a breathless moment she felt like a schoolgirl in the throes of her first mindless passion. Without warning, a flood of gladness swept through her, and the day became even brighter. Before she had time to evaluate the tide of emotions that were quickening her breathing, the bell-like tone of the hunting horn and the "talley-ho" of the huntmaster sang through the air.

As though released from a cage, the twenty or so riders took off, bruising riders all. The first part of the course was fairly easy—the fields were clear of trees and bushes, and the fences and hedges were fairly low. The belling of the hounds left a trail for the hallooing riders to follow. The pack veered through a small wood where riding was somewhat more hazardous.

Amelia had fully entered into the spirit of the ride. She felt like a mythical goddess as she rode to the chase atop the fleetest of steeds. The sound of her exultant laughter trailed behind her to reach Justin's ears, exciting in him a similar exultation. The trees of the grove thinned out, and the course became more rocky. Despite the strength of Amelia's horse, the rest of the hunt had pulled ahead; soon she and Justin were separated from the rest of the riders.

Amelia exhorted her horse to go faster.

The great horse gathered himself for a greater effort. Horse and rider seemed to fly across the ground. Once again Amelia's laughter trilled behind her, joyous and free. She felt cut loose from the bonds that tied her to her obligations and responsibilities; for the moment she was like the wind, blowing swift and clean.

Once more the course was intersected by walls and hedges. As horse and rider approached the first obstruction, Amelia gathered up the reins and leaned forward to urge Signore to further effort. The animal mustered himself for the jump, tucking his forelegs up as he sprang with the full strength of his hindquarters. His front legs moved forward in the rhythm of his stride as he cleared the wall and began his landing. But without warning, just as his right hoof struck the ground, it broke through the soil into a mole's tunnel. There was no way he could recover from the brutal shock of the misstep; as he fell forward, his leg snapped.

To the earl, who was a hundred yards or more behind Amelia, it was as though rider and mount had vanished. He heard the sound of the horse as the leg broke, the thud of the body, and then silence, broken only by the distant ululation of the hounds as they ran the fox to earth and the pound of his horse's hooves. There was no sound from Amelia.

Farnham reined in his animal as they came up to the wall. He jumped off and clambered over the rocks, calling for Amelia in a frantic voice. The sight he saw made him turn pale. The cream-colored mount was struggling to rise, his coat covered with soil and debris, and blood streaming from the broken skin of his leg. Ten feet beyond the animal lay the still form of the woman Farnham loved. Her skin was pale, and a trickle of blood stained her forehead. Justin ran to her, fearing the worst; she lay so still and lifeless, almost without breathing. Only when the earl had placed his hand to the barely moving breast was he assured that she still lived.

"Thank God . . . Amelia . . . Amelia . . ." He gently touched her face, trying to recall her to consciousness. He ripped the cravat from around his neck and used the material to wipe away the blood from her skin, then carefully bound the wound with the linen.

"Oh, my sweet love, please live. God, where are the other riders? I can't leave her alone here." Justin divested himself of his riding coat and placed it over Amelia, tucking it around her in an attempt to protect her from the cold ground. The day, which just a few minutes before had seemed so bright and cheerful, had suddenly taken on a malignant cast. As he kneeled beside the stricken woman, he heard the sound of hoofbeats approaching.

He rose to his feet, calling out, "Hoy! Here we are! Help!"

A groom who had been guiding a string of fresh horses toward the distant riders dismounted and ran over to the wall. "What happened, sir? Is the lady . . . Has she . . ."

"No, she's alive, but she's still unconscious. I don't know how badly injured she is." The earl ran back to Amelia. "You'll have to help me lift her over the wall. I can't leave her here, it's too cold."

The groom interrupted him. "There's a break in the wall just a little ways over there, sir," he said, pointing to his right. "I could take the horses around and, once you're mounted, hand her up to you. Be much easier than lifting her twice."

"You're right, bring my horse around. You don't have a gun with you, do you?"

"You mean for him, sir?" The groom gestured at the struggling horse. "I'm that sorry, sir. We don't normally carry firearms with us unless there's a reason for't. Poor brute. It'll be a while till we can put him out of his misery."

"Yes, well, hurry up then. I've got to get Mrs. Carrington back to the house. She'll need a doctor."

The groom remounted after tying the other horses to some bushes and quickly took off for the break in the wall. The earl kneeled down beside Amelia, once more speaking to her as though she could hear him. "My dearest, dearest delight, don't leave me now. I have such a need for you."

He bent down to slide his arms under her, lifting her from the ground. Her white face was empty of the vivacious spirit and lively intelligence that normally brightened her countenance. As the earl stood, tenderly cradling her in his arms, her long tresses loosened from her hat, curled and clung to the brown superfine of his riding coat. There was no trace of color in her cheeks. The ribbon of blood from the wound at her temple accented the pallor of her skin.

Still murmuring endearments and pleas to her to waken, the earl touched her face with his lips. "You mustn't die, Amelia. I won't let you. We're going to have a long and happy life together before you meet your maker." The distraught man turned his face to the sky in a silent plea.

"My lord." Jamison had ridden up, unnoticed by the earl. "If you would give me the lady, I'll hold her while you mount and then hand her up to you. I think we should try to get her back as fast as possible."

"All right, move your horse down this little slope. We'll be more on an even keel then." Farnham was standing on a slight rise of the land. "Here, take her carefully. Hold her easy, while I mount up." Quickly, the earl seated himself on his chestnut hunter and moved to the side of the waiting groom. Amelia was gently transferred to his arms.

"Now, ride as fast as you can. Have the doctor called for and tell Mrs. Carrington's maid to have her bed readied with extra warming pans." Farnham gave his orders in a crisp voice. "I shall have to ride more slowly to avoid jolting the lady. Don't bother with the other horses. You'll have to arrange for someone to fetch them and deal with her poor beast. They'll be all right for now. And thank you, Jamison." Justin's voice softened. "I don't know what I would have done without you."

As the groom wheeled his horse around and started for the chase at a gallop, the earl tightened his hold on Amelia and chirruped to his horse, guiding him with his knees.

CHAPTER TWENTY

By THE TIME Justin arrived at the side entrance to the chase, a crowd of servants were waiting to give what help they could. Annie and Staunton ran to his side, Staunton reaching up to take Amelia's still form from the earl.

"My little Melly, what have you done to yourself, my pet?" Annie moaned upon seeing Amelia's silent figure. "She's not...she's not dead, is she?"

"Don't be foolish," Staunton told her before the earl could respond. "Melly's got many a year to go before you'll be able to say that of her. Here, my lord, give her into my arms so you can get yourself down."

Reluctantly Justin leaned over with his fragile burden, gently lowering her into Staunton's waiting grasp. Lightly he jumped from the back of his mount and took the unconscious woman from her grizzled servitor.

"Have you warmed her bed? Has anyone been sent for the doctor?" Justin threw questions at Annie and Staunton as they followed him up the stairway. As he reached the landing, Annie ran ahead to open the door to Amelia's room and then helped the earl to place her upon the bed. "Call me as soon as you've undressed her. I wish to stay with her until the doctor arrives."

Annie, shocked by the anguished tone of Farnham's voice, quickly agreed to his order. As soon as he left the room, she began to chafe Amelia's hands, trying to arouse her. Frightened by the chill of those hands, she unfastened the heavy velvet riding habit, cutting the fabric away from the still body so as not to disturb Amelia more than absolutely necessary. She wrapped her in a fleecy robe, placed the warming pans at her feet, and covered her with blankets.

Breathing a prayer, Annie went to the door to inform the earl that her Melly was tucked into her bed.

"As soon as the doctor arrives, send him up. I shall stay with her until then." Annie could almost swear that the earl's eyes held a hint of tears. "I don't want her left alone for a moment."

"She'll come through this, my lord. She's a lot of strength has Melly—Mrs. Carrington, that is. Why don't you sit yourself down on this chair next to the bed. I'm sure she'll be all right." Annie suddenly saw the haughty nobleman with more kindly eyes. She was sure now that he loved Amelia with the same depth of feeling that her dearie felt for him. If only she would come through this terrible accident, then her future would be set.

The earl seated himself as Annie had suggested. He moved the chair until he was able to touch Amelia's hand, which he lifted to his lips, pressing a kiss to the soft skin.

"You know, Amelia, I think I've always loved you. You must live so that I can tell you that a thousand times. We've lost so much time already. I don't want to lose more. Think of us, sweetheart, Perry and me. We both need you and love you." Justin lay his head on the coverlet next to Amelia's still body. Never had he felt so helpless; never had he concentrated his will so fiercely.

He was still in that position when the doctor arrived an hour later. Only the slight flutter of breath moving Amelia's nostrils gave proof that she lived. The tired man lifted his head at the sound of the doctor's hearty voice.

"My lord, I'm Dr. Farraday. Your man told me the lady was thrown from a horse and injured her head?"

"Yes, almost two hours ago, and she hasn't awakened since then. She seems to have struck her head on a stone when she landed. She's not even moved. Is it possible she's paralyzed?"

"We won't know until she regains consciousness, my lord. It's not unusual for a victim of such an accident to remain unconscious for several hours. Almost as though the body needs that period of rest to overcome the damage to the nervous system. The humors of the blood, y'know." The doctor tried to reassure the earl.

"What do you mean, the humors of the blood?"

"Well, my lord, even though we've learned much about the circulation of the blood, there's still so much we don't know." The doctor began what looked to be a long and involved exposition on the practice of medicine as he knew it.

"You mean you don't know any more than I do about her condition," the earl interrupted the speech.

The medical man paused, obviously shocked by the earl's attack. "My lord, I . . . you're right. I only know that she should have rest and quiet. She may show some confusion when she comes to her senses. Don't let her be upset or interrogated. She must have no excitement, plenty of fluids, and a very light diet. No more than two people should attend her at any time." Dr. Farraday offered some hope to Justin. "It's not unusual for this deep unconsciousness to follow a blow such as she seems to have sustained. I've seen men take the same and in three or four days be fully recovered. I'm sorry that I can't offer you more."

"Thank you, Doctor. I . . . forgive me for being so hard on you." Justin smiled ruefully at the man as he made his apology.

The doctor patted him on the back. "That's all right." He carefully removed the cravat to examine Amelia's forehead, then cleaned and bandaged it. "I'll look in on Mrs. Carrington tomorrow. When the lady wakens, she will probably have a headache of the worst order. A cool compress will be helpful and a dose of laudanum. And keep her calm. Good-bye, my lord."

Again Justin thanked the doctor and bid him farewell. He moved about the bedchamber, examining and touching Amelia's personal belongings. The silver-backed hand mirror that rested on the *poudoir* had her initials entwined on the back. Next to it lay a strand of pearls that she had worn the evening before. He lifted them to his face, thinking that the rosy color of the pearls was no more beautiful than the rosy glow of her cheeks.

On a chair near the window lay a scarf, tossed carelessly down some time before. He crushed the fabric in his hands, holding it up to his nostrils, breathing deeply of the scent that was Amelia's. As he stood with his head bowed over the material, he heard the hunters returning from the chase. The sounds were almost immediately muted; Annie or Staunton must have suggested that the returning guests be asked to speak quietly. Within minutes there was a soft tap at the door.

Slowly the earl let the fragrant scarf fall back to the chair as Eglantine slipped into the room.

"Oh, Justin, I'm so sorry. I heard . . . what happened?" she whispered. "How did she get hurt?"

Quietly and quickly, Justin explained what had happened. Despite his attempt to be reassuring about Amelia's recovery, his anxiety was apparent. Before Tina could question him further, he asked her to explain the need for quiet in the house to the rest of the party and that they excuse him from joining with them in their activities until Amelia had recovered.

"I have no desire to be elsewhere than beside her, Eglantine. I only hope I haven't waited too long to discover my love for her. I don't think I would want to live if she is not able to share my life with me."

"Hush, Justin, don't talk like that." Lady Winterset was shocked by the intensity of Justin's distress. "It may take awhile, but I'm sure she'll be all right. Has anyone told Perry that his mother has been injured?"

"No, there's no need to tell him until we know that she's recovering. I don't wish the boy to have to go through any kind of ordeal now. I'll speak to Annie about talking to him when I can tell him something hopeful. Why should he have to sit a vigil? He's too young to understand what's happening."

Eglantine agreed that Perry should be protected from the news about his mother's illness and left the room murmuring to Justin that Amelia was too good for them to lose her.

Justin sat down once more next to Amelia. He gazed intently at her dear face, remembering the many expressions he had watched with both delight and anger; her smile when she had successfully made a point the afternoon they had spent with the travelers at the inn; the pout when she thought he had teased her too strenuously the morning after Perry's pony ran away with him; the joy when she had blazed with love in his arms.

"Oh, Amelia, I love you so." He rested his head against her side.

"Justin..." A whisper of sound reached his ear as a feather touch caressed his hair.

Incredulous, he lifted his head, not believing what his heart hoped for. Amelia's hand touched his cheek lightly as he moved. "How did I get here? What happened?" Her voice was a thin sound in the room. "My head...aches so."

"Oh, my dearest, I thought never to hear you again." Justin leaned down to place a delicate kiss on Amelia's lips. "Your horse stumbled and threw you badly; your head hit a rock and you've been unconscious these past several hours. I was so afraid for you...."

"I thought you didn't care what happened to me. Sit down and let me hold your hand. I don't feel very well." She raised her hand to her head and felt the bandage for the first time. "What's this? Why do I have a bandage on my head?"

"The skin was cut a bit when you struck the stone. Don't

worry, the doctor said you should not be concerned about it. You mustn't talk, and you must have rest. Annie will give you some laudanum for the pain in a few minutes."

The earl smiled tenderly at his love. "At last I can tell you something that I've been wanting you to know for days. First I must beg your forgiveness for the way I treated you that morning when I discovered who you were. If you find it difficult to acquit me of that misdeed, permit me to say that I wish only to care for you and Perry for the rest of my life. I love you, Amelia—more than I ever thought I could love anyone. I loved my lady of mystery and, had she given me the opportunity, would have married her. Of course that was impossible then, but now please say you will do me that honor. Put your life in my hands. I will make it more beautiful than anything you have ever known."

"Oh, Justin, how I've longed to hear you say that! I never let myself believe we could have a life together. Please, help me sit up." Amelia lifted her head from the pillow to look entreatingly at the earl.

"It's too soon. The doctor—"

"Please, I want you to put your arms around me. Shall I tell you I will faint if you don't heed me?" Despite her weakness, Amelia was not beyond teasing him. "How can you not do as I ask when you have just told me you love me so much?"

"I think you're feeling more yourself." At last the earl grinned at Amelia. "I do this under protest, you understand, although I want nothing more at this moment than to hold you." Carefully he slipped an arm under her shoulders and raised her to a sitting position. Still holding her, he sat down beside her and enveloped her in his arms, lifting her to his lap as though she were a small child. "There, now I have you, and I promise I shall never let you go."

"Just don't bounce me about. I am becoming too familiar with my head; the joggling has an ill effect on it." She rested her head against his chest, letting the beat of his heart comfort her. "I feel as though I have come home, to be resting in your arms like this."

"I am your home, sweet love, as you shall learn more

and more in our life together. Does your head hurt too much for you to lift it so I can kiss you? I feel I must drink from your lips before another moment passes." The kiss that Justin placed on Amelia's lips, as gentle as a breath, held more love and promise than any more passionate kiss they had ever shared. "With this kiss I thee betroth," he pronounced softly, "and make you mine."

"Dearest Justin, I believe I'm almost glad that I had that fall, if that's what it took to bring us together." Amelia breathed happily into his shirtfront. "I must be dreaming. How can everything change so suddenly? Are you sure?"

"The change wasn't sudden, my love. I've known for a while that you are my only love, but you treated me with such coldness. You showed such a partiality for Sir Richard that I thought you would never listen to my suit." He lifted her hand to his lips for a quick caress. "I couldn't tell you, not even that I was coming to love Perry; that I was thrilled to know he is my son. We have a lot of time to make up, Amelia." Justin finally responded to the two arms that had crept around his neck, and once more he met Amelia's lips with his in a seeking, passionate kiss.

When finally she pulled her mouth from his, her shining green eyes gave him her promise of love. So absorbed were they in their newly made commitment that neither heard the door to the chamber open.

"Why are you hugging my mama? You're not supposed to be here with her." The indignant voice of a small boy made itself heard. "Let go of her this minute, or I shall call for Staunton!"

The two adults, startled by the unexpected interruption, turned to see a gap-toothed gladiator ready to do battle to save his mother.

"A moment, dearest, while I deal with this very brave son," Justin murmured to Amelia. He removed her arms from around his neck and helped her to lie down. Calmly he reached for his son, drawing him to his side, inspecting the sturdy child's face. What he saw there was a lessening of outrage and a return of the trust that had been his prior to this meeting. "I have something very important to ask you, Perry. It's true that you're a bit young to make such a momentous decision, but I trust your judgment. After all, we have spoken about some very weighty matters in the past few days, and you seem able to make good, solid decisions."

Perry gravely accepted the earl's evaluation, not quite understanding the import of all the words. He stood silently, studying first Farnham's face and then Amelia's. When he saw that his mother was not frightened or averse to this man's presence, he nodded his head.

"I've never asked for anyone's hand, let alone asked permission from a six-year-old." The earl shrugged, smiled at Amelia, and proceeded to address Perry. "Perry, I have come to regard your mother and yourself most highly. In fact, I would like you to live with me. That is to say, not just live with me, but I would like your mother to become my wife and you to become my son. Your mother has said she would like that above all things. Do you think you would also?" Justin was caught between laughing and crying at the thought that such a child, in fact his son, should hold the future happiness of the Earl of Croyville in his hands. If Perry refused, it went without saying that Amelia would ignore her own happiness for that of her child. The time until Perry finally worded his answer seemed to last a million years.

"You mean you want to be my papa? And I can be with you always? Oh, that would be of all things top of the mark." The child looked at Justin with shining eyes and an expectant grin. "There's to be a balloonist coming. Staunton told me so. Now you can take me, true?"

A hearty laugh escaped Justin. "Scamp! Yes, now I can take you, and your mother as soon as she's up to it!" He wrapped his arms about Perry and gave him the hug that had been waiting to be bestowed ever since he had discovered the child's true identity. Then, still holding the boy in the curve of his right arm, he once more lifted Amelia into his left and, hugging mother and son tightly to him, he announced his intention to make them the happiest mother and son ever to be found in England.

EPILOGUE

SLOWLY THE LAUGHING wedding guests moved back into the ballroom of Croyville, shivering in the winter air. The wedding celebration had been one of the gayest, happiest events attended by the many friends of the newly married Lord and Lady Croyville. The ceremony had taken place in the ancient Croyville chapel, a simple, moving ritual in which the bride and groom spoke their vows with depth and sincerity. Amelia Carrington, wearing an ivory velvet gown bordered in white mink, was accompanied by her son, who acted as Lord Croyville's page, handing him the heavy gold wedding band at the proper time. There was such a feeling of love between the child, his mother, and his "adoptive" father that the spectators were warmed by the reflection.

Lord Croyville had hardly let his lady leave his side until it had been time for her to don her traveling clothes, and then he had disappeared with Perry, the two of them returning wearing similar jackets, pantaloons, and boots. The resemblance between the two had been noted by some of those present, but only three or four of those knew the truth of the relationship. The others thought it likely that Amelia's first husband had dark coloring. When Amelia had appeared, there had been a final toast to the health and happiness of the bride and groom, accompanied by laughter at the unconventionality of taking a six-year-old child along with them on their honeymoon.

Annie and Staunton stood on the steps waving to the departing carriage until not even the dust of its passage could be seen. As Annie wiped the tears from her cheeks, she turned to Staunton and said, "I didn't think it could be brought off, but thanks to Lady Winterset and just plain good luck, our Melly is married to the man she's loved all along. Do you think Mr. Alfred ever knew?"

"I think he knew right enough as soon as he heard she was expecting a child. But he was an unusual man, Annie. He trusted her even though he suspected the child wasn't his." Staunton put his arm around Annie. "He was a fine man, was Mr. Carrington, and when he made up that plan for Melly to follow, I think he was hoping she'd find Perry's real father and marry up with him just as she has."

"Now she'll have everything he would have wanted for her—her man to love and care for her and the child. Oh, I shall miss them while they're away. There's naught for us to do here. With all the servants, there's no place for us."

"Well, luv, we could go back to London. No need to stay here. The lease on the Princess Gardens don't run out for months yet." Staunton turned Annie to face him. "What do you say, Annie? Our job's done. Don't you think it's our turn now, m'dearie?" He laughed at the open-mouthed expression on Annie's face. "How's about it then? We're not too old to enjoy a few years of that there wedded bliss."

And, reader, they did.

WATCH FOR
6 NEW TITLES EVERY MONTH!

Second Chance at Love

____ 06318-5 **SAPPHIRE ISLAND #27** Diane Crawford

____ 06335-5 **APHRODITE'S LEGEND #28** Lynn Fairfax

____ 06336-3 **TENDER TRIUMPH #29** Jasmine Craig

____ 06280-4 **AMBER-EYED MAN #30** Johanna Phillips

____ 06249-9 **SUMMER LACE #31** Jenny Nolan

____ 06305-3 **HEARTTHROB #32** Margarett McKean

____ 05626-X **AN ADVERSE ALLIANCE #33** Lucia Curzon

____ 06162-X **LURED INTO DAWN #34** Catherine Mills

____ 06195-6 **SHAMROCK SEASON #35** Jennifer Rose

____ 06304-5 **HOLD FAST TIL MORNING #36** Beth Brookes

____ 06282-0 **HEARTLAND #37** Lynn Fairfax

____ 06408-4 **FROM THIS DAY FORWARD #38** Jolene Adams

____ 05968-4 **THE WIDOW OF BATH #39** Anne Devon

All titles $1.75

Available at your local bookstore or return this form to:

SECOND CHANCE AT LOVE
The Berkley/Jove Publishing Group
200 Madison Avenue, New York, New York 10016

**Please enclose 50¢ for postage and handling for one book, 25¢
each add'l book ($1.25 max.). No cash, CODs or stamps. Total
amount enclosed: $ _____ in check or money order.**

NAME _____

ADDRESS _____

CITY _____ STATE/ZIP _____

Allow six weeks for delivery.   SK-41

QUESTIONNAIRE

1. How many romances do you *read* each month? _____

2. How many of these do you *buy* each month? _____

3. Do you read primarily
   - ☐ novels in romance lines like SECOND CHANCE AT LOVE
   - ☐ historical romances
   - ☐ bestselling contemporary romances
   - ☐ other _____

4. Were the love scenes in this novel (this is book # _____)
   - ☐ too explicit
   - ☐ not explicit enough
   - ☐ tastefully handled

5. On what basis do you make your decision to buy a romance?
   - ☐ friend's recommendation
   - ☐ bookseller's recommendation
   - ☐ art on the front cover
   - ☐ description of the plot on the back cover
   - ☐ author
   - ☐ other _____

6. Where did you buy this book?
   - ☐ chain store (drug, department, etc.)
   - ☐ bookstore
   - ☐ supermarket
   - ☐ other _____

7. Mind telling your age?
   - ☐ under 18
   - ☐ 18 to 30
   - ☐ 31 to 45
   - ☐ over 45

8. How many SECOND CHANCE AT LOVE novels have you read?
   - ☐ this is the first
   - ☐ some (give number, please _____)

9. How do you rate SECOND CHANCE AT LOVE vs. competing lines?
   - ☐ poor
   - ☐ fair
   - ☐ good
   - ☐ excellent

10. Check here if you would like to
   - ☐ receive the SECOND CHANCE AT LOVE Newsletter

. . . .

Fill-in your name and address below:

name:_____

street address:_____

city_____ state_____ zip_____

Please share your other ideas about romances with us on an additional sheet and attach it securely to this questionnaire.

PLEASE RETURN THIS QUESTIONNAIRE TO:
SECOND CHANCE AT LOVE, THE BERKLEY/JOVE PUBLISHING GROUP
200 Madison Avenue, New York, New York 10016